SUBMISSION

DOMS OF CLUB EDEN

LK SHAW

Submission, Doms of Club Eden Book 1

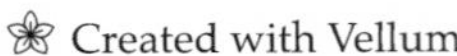
Created with Vellum

WANT A FREE SHORT STORY? Be sure to sign up for my newsletter and download your copy of A Birthday Spanking, a Doms of Club Eden prequel! http://eepurl.com/ds5MOb

AVAILABLE IN KINDLE UNLIMITED

Doms of Club Eden

Submission

Desire

Redemption

Protect

Betrayal

My Christmas Dom

Covert Liaisons Series

Love Undercover

Striking Distance (Coming 2019)

Atonement (Coming 2020)

Other Books

SEALs in Love

Say Yes

CHAPTER 1

"YOU CAN DO THIS," I muttered to myself while I peeped out my car windshield. With a deep exhale, I wiped my sweaty palms on my pant leg and tried to calm the butterflies in my belly. I could feel my heart beating in my ears. I'd been sitting here for thirty minutes. I looked down at the ridiculous container of store-bought potato salad. It was probably getting warm. And gross.

I caught movement out of my periphery. Just a couple walking to their car. I didn't know what I hoped to see from my parking space way in the back. The longer I sat there, though, the greater the urge was to leave. But damn it, I'd come this far. What could it hurt to mingle a little? I mean, these were just normal people, right? Kinky people, but still totally normal. Except for me. I was as vanilla as they came. Or was I? That's what I was here to find out.

Now or never. With that, I quickly grabbed the stupid plastic tub and exited my car before I changed my mind. With a determined stride, I made my way across the parking lot and up the sidewalk toward the shelter house.

My steps stuttered briefly when heads turned at my entrance. I gave an awkward smile and set my offering in an empty space between a tin pan of burnt hot dogs and a mostly empty baking dish of what looked like macaroni and cheese.

When I turned back around, no one was paying me any attention. Trying to remain inconspicuous, I stepped off to the side to stand against the wall, observing those sitting at the picnic tables scattered around.

"Well, who do we have here?" A deep, gravelly voice at my right drew my attention. My breath hitched and my body heated when I spotted the sexiest man I'd ever laid eyes on. I'd always been a sucker for a man with salt and pepper hair. Damn, he filled out that navy t-shirt nicely. My eyes traveled his full length before returning to his face. I flushed at the amused half-smile he wore at my perusal. It took me a moment to remember he'd asked me a question.

"Pe-Penny," I stuttered, almost breathless as the heat in my face intensified. I don't remember blushing this much before in my life. *Fake it 'til you make it* was my mantra. I stood a little taller and attempted to gain the confidence I typically displayed with chauvinistic surgeons.

"I'm Marcus." His secret smile remained as he reached out to shake my hand. When I placed mine in his, he squeezed it firmly, and I thought I felt his thumb gently caress mine, but he pulled away before I could be sure.

"Nice to meet you." The words came out a little shaky.

"So, what brings you out to play with us today?" His voice dropped suggestively.

Maintaining my barely-there confidence, I answered his question. "I'm curious about domination and submission. I figured this was the best place to gain some knowledge."

"Knowledge about what?" Marcus asked, showing true interest.

Everything. I wanted to know what it felt like to give up control.

To just feel and not have to think.

To be dominated.

To have someone fulfill needs I didn't even know I had.

I wanted to find my happily ever after, damn it. Sadly, I didn't know how to express any of this.

I shrugged my shoulders. "Whatever someone will teach me."

"Sweetness," he murmured, "I'd be happy to teach you anything you want to know. In the meantime, why don't I introduce you to some friends of mine."

With a hand across my lower back, startling me with the sparks of electricity that flowed through my extremities, Marcus led me over to a group of women.

"Ladies, I'd like to introduce you to Penny. This is her first munch. She's here getting the lay of the land, so to speak. I have no doubt you'll make her feel welcome." There was an undercurrent of command in his tone.

I sat on the bench and Marcus moved away. The back of my neck tingled like I was still being watched, but I ignored the sensation.

"Hi, I'm Bridget."

My eyes landed on a gorgeous redhead with chocolate-colored eyes and a bright, welcoming smile that seemed genuine. She looked about my age. She continued introducing the rest of the group while she pointed at each woman who waved when she spoke their name.

"That's Delilah, Jackie, and Priscilla, but we call her Priss."

"Nice to meet you."

"Soooo," she drew out the word, "I assume you're a sub?"

"Um, I'm not really sure."

She laughed. "Well, if you're not, then Marcus there is going to be sadly disappointed."

My face heated.

"He hasn't taken his eyes off you since the moment you sat down." This came from Delilah.

"I'm sure he's just making sure everyone is having a good time." I tried brushing off their words.

They all continued to stare at me in a placating way.

Bridget spoke up. "If you say so."

I quickly changed the topic. "So, are there munches held very often?"

Thankfully, they let the previous topic go. "We have a munch at The Local Cue on the first Friday of every month."

"The Local Cue?" I asked Priss, I think her name was.

"It's a billiards club over on Hamilton Street."

Bridget chimed in. "You should totally come next week."

We continued talking for the next hour or so. I learned so much listening to them talk about their lifestyle. It was fascinating. Soon though, the potluck was winding down, and I needed to get going.

"Thank you all for making me feel welcome. I debating getting out of my car for over thirty minutes, and I'm so glad I did. This was fun. I'm definitely going to come on Friday."

Bridget stood when I did, and I was surprised when she pulled me into a hug.

"It was so nice to meet you. I really do hope you'll come this weekend. We have so much fun and there are a ton of people I can introduce you to. We're an open and accepting group. Let me give you my phone number. If you ever have any questions about anything or just want someone to talk to, give me a call."

We exchanged phone numbers and I waved goodbye to everyone. I hadn't made it five feet before a sinful voice stopped me.

"Have you discovered any deep, dark secrets yet?" Marcus asked.

"Yours or mine?" I slowly turned to face him.

Marcus stepped closer and closer, edging me backward until I was flush with the wall behind me. The wall where this day began. He stopped just short of touching me. Instead, he leaned down, his warm breath caressing my ear.

"Why, yours, of course. I'm curious to know what depraved secrets you keep buried that you wish someone like me would discover. In fact, I think I would enjoy that immensely. Discovering your secrets, that is. Secrets I'm going to bet involve all the scandalous things you've fantasized about. A man binding your hands above your head while he feasts on your your sweet, succulent cunt."

I whimpered at the picture he painted, and my knees almost gave out. He was right. I did have those fantasies. I had to brace myself against the cement at my back.

He continued when he sensed my arousal. "You want to be fucked harder than you've ever been fucked before.

Your ass spanked. You want to come like you've never come before."

Every scene flashed through my mind and god did I want it. I wanted everything he described. It terrified me this ecstasy flowing through me. I didn't even know this man, but I had a feeling that if, given the chance, he'd discover all my secrets.

Overwhelmed by the onslaught, I gasped. "I have to go."

CHAPTER 2

My eyes followed the departure of one of the sexiest women I'd ever seen. I knew I'd come on strong, but it was like I couldn't stop the words from flowing. I didn't regret them, though. Every utterance was true. When I'd seen her standing alone, her luscious curves so utterly tempting, I was compelled to go and meet her. She hadn't looked familiar to me, and I knew most everyone in the BDSM community in Pinegrove. I'd been shocked to discover she had no clue the submissive vibes she gave off. Her nervous curiosity was sweet. And oh so sexy.

"You scared her off, didn't you? God, you're such a man."

Now that Penny was out of view, I turned to find Bridget standing there with hands on her hips.

"You're lucky we're at a vanilla event, Bridge, or I might decide a punishment is in order. You know how I feel about brats."

She scoffed, ever fearless. "With all due respect, Marcus, you're not my Dom."

Ignoring her, I strode toward my friend, and fellow Dom, Connor, knowing Bridget would be right behind me. She was opinionated and didn't care who knew it. I didn't envy the Dom who would eventually tame her. I enjoyed spirit and fire, but not a brat.

"I liked her. What did you say that had her practically running out of here?"

I cut Bridget a little slack. While sometimes more mouthy than I could handle, she was a fiercely loyal friend who had helped me at a time I desperately needed it. What she'd done was more than I could ever repay.

"I flirted a little." I threw over my shoulder while her legs quickly ate up the distance between us.

"Who did you flirt with?" Connor spoke up from his lounge chair. I took the empty seat next to him and picked up the glass of lemonade I'd abandoned earlier. Bridget remained standing over the two of us, her foot tapping impatiently. She didn't wait for me to respond. Instead, in typical Bridget fashion she barreled ahead.

"Her name is Penny. She was new here today and after this guy got all up in her personal space and whispered who knows what to her, she hustled out of here like her ass was on fire. So, whatever he said to her went beyond a little flirting. I know how he flirts. Probably said something overly sexual."

Guilty heat crept up the back of my neck.

"For fuck's sake Marcus, you're going to scare all the newbies away," Connor grumbled.

I glared at them both. "She wasn't scared. Don't worry, she'll be back."

"Well, I'm going to call her later and make sure you

didn't fuck things up just in case." With those parting words, Bridget turned and stomped off.

I took another sip of my drink before turning to Connor. To my surprise, his eyes remained on the retreating woman, and there was a spark of longing there I'd never seen before. When he caught me watching him, his expression quickly shuttered.

"So, what did you want to talk to me about?" he redirected the conversation. *Interesting*.

Regardless of whatever was going on between him and Bridget, it was none of my business, so I refrained from asking any questions. Besides, what I needed to discuss was more important.

"I got another letter from Evan."

"Fuck, again?" Connor slammed his fist on his arm rest. "I've had my best team working on finding that son of a bitch, so I don't understand how he's been able to remain in hiding. The minute I think we've located him, he disappears. You didn't happen to bring it with you?"

I shook my head. "It's on my desk at home. I was planning on bringing it to your office tomorrow."

"I'm there by seven, so stop by any time. What did he say this time?"

"The same thing he always says. How it's only a matter of time before he finds Grace. That she'll regret ever leaving him. That he'll make me pay for keeping her from him."

Connor shook his head. "He has to have someone helping him if Josie can't even find him. She's fucking brilliant and the best IT person I know."

"Then, whoever it is, you better find him. Before Evan

does discover where she is. If anything happens to either of them, there's no law that will stop me from killing him."

"It's not going to come to that. We'll find him."

Connor was one of my best friends, and I trusted him with my life. And other's lives. But the fact remained, Evan Banks was dangerous and smart, a lethal combination. "I hope so."

"Josie will find him, Marcus," he repeated more firmly this time.

I merely nodded. We sat in silence for several minutes before Connor broke it. "So, tell me about this woman you allegedly ran off with your flirting."

A groan rumbled up from my chest. "I didn't run her off. She was already leaving."

"Regardless, from the sounds of things you hurried her along."

I flipped him off. "I wanted her to know I found her attractive. Maybe I went a little overboard, but I got my point across."

Connor chuckled and took a small swig of his drink. "I'm sure you did. Do you think she'll be back?"

I couldn't help but smile with a hint of self-satisfaction. "Oh, she'll be back. Bridget will make sure of it. Speaking of. You gonna tell me about it?"

His expression went completely blank. "Nothing to tell."

I studied him intently and he didn't so much as flinch. Respecting his request I gave up my questioning.

"You got it."

After taking the final swallow of my now warm lemonade, I rose from my chair. "See you at Eden tonight?"

Connor saluted me with his cup. "Like always."

"Sounds good."

I said goodbye to a few more people before heading home, the curvy auburn-haired beauty never far from my thoughts.

CHAPTER 3

My eyes darted to the clock, my body riding a wave of excitement and nervousness. Finally, it was time to head to the munch. To see Marcus. Not that I was going there strictly for him. I ignored the voice in my head calling me a liar, especially since I'd done nothing but think of him all week. Hell, I'd even pulled out my vibrator twice and got myself off picturing him doing all the dirty things he had described to me before I rushed off. My core throbbed just thinking about it.

I took one final glance at myself in the mirror. Wanting to look cute, but also not like I was trying too hard to impress anyone, I'd spent thirty minutes going through my closet debating what I was going to wear. I finally decided on a purple, one-shouldered, crocheted dress that fell mid-thigh, hugged my curves, and disguised my belly roll. The silver peep-toe pumps finished off the outfit. I quickly dabbed my favorite perfume between my breasts and behind my ears before I grabbed my purse and headed out the door.

A short drive later, I entered the pool hall and instantly scanned the faces I saw, hoping to find the green eyes I hadn't stopped thinking about. It took me less than two minutes before I zeroed in on Marcus. He lounged against the opposite wall talking to three other men. I studied him for several minutes. He laughed freely making him look several years younger. My eyes tracked a path down his body. His exposed forearms were perfectly muscled, and his dark-washed jeans left little to the imagination.

When my gaze returned to his face, it was to find him staring back at me with a sensual half-smile ticking up one side of his mouth. Immediately, a throbbing began between my legs, and my nipples hardened. I couldn't bring myself to tear my eyes away. A loud feminine laugh drew my vision away from him, and I spotted Bridget. Using her as an excuse to gather my composure, I hastily made my way over.

Thankfully she spotted me and a huge smile graced her face as she waved. "Yay, you made it. Have you been here long?"

She pulled me into a hug. "No, I just got here actually."

"Well come on, let's go get you a drink then."

We stepped away from the group she'd been with and headed to the mostly empty bar.

The bartender, whose name tag read Grant, stepped over to us flipping a towel over his shoulder. "What can I get you ladies?"

"I'll take a sex on the beach." Bridget winked at the good-looking man.

"A whiskey sour for me, please."

"You got it," Grant nodded before stepping away to fill our order.

Bridget turned toward me. "Have you seen Marcus yet?"

My cheeks heated. "Briefly, when I first walked in."

When I didn't say anything more, she prodded. "And? Did he see you?"

Damn, she was relentless. "We made eye contact. I saw you, and here we are."

She shook her head sadly. "Woman, we need to work on your flirting skills. Lord, it's like you two were made for each other. His flirting skills are ridiculously sexual and yours seem to be non-existent."

"Hey," I countered, mildly offended even though she was right. "I'm new to this whole lifestyle. Maybe flirting is different here. I feel so out of place."

Bridget was immediately contrite. "Oh, shit, I'm sorry. I wasn't trying to be an asshole. I was just giving you a hard time. You are not out of place, so don't even think that. We were all new at one time. Flirting in the BDSM community isn't any different than in the vanilla community except we have safe words. If you're not interested in Marcus, that's okay. But I should tell you, he's one of the nicest men you'll ever meet."

Just then, Grant returned with our drinks. "One sex on the beach and one whiskey sour."

As I took a sip of mine I became curious, and not to mention a little jealous, about something that just occurred to me. I was hesitant to ask because I didn't want to know the answer. I asked it anyway. "Have you two ever…"

Bridget reared back with an almost horrified look on her face. "Lord, no. I mean, yes, but no. We've played a few times, but it was merely for the power exchange, not the sex."

The complete confusion I was feeling must have been on my face because she went on. "He's topped me so I could submit and expunge my emotions and shit, but we've never had sex."

I still didn't really understand what she was saying, but hearing that Marcus had never had sex with Bridget made me feel unexpectedly better.

"Would you have been jealous if she and I had?" The deep, gravely voice came from over my right shoulder.

I spun around, my hand on my chest trying to quiet my racing heart. "You scared the shit out of me. And to answer your question, no I wouldn't have been jealous."

Marcus smirked like he didn't believe me.

"I'm going to leave you two to chat. Call me later."

"Bridg…" I sputtered, but she'd already walked away. I stared at her back when suddenly she turned half-way around, smiled, and waggled her eyebrows at me. I huffed and glared at Marcus, who smothered a laugh with a cough.

"You'll get used to her after a while." He shrugged. "Now, where were we? Oh, yes, you were denying any jealousy." He took two steps forward.

"Are you sure about that?" his breath fanned across my face. It smelled like peppermint. My favorite flavor.

I straightened my shoulders. "Yes, I'm sure. I mean, I don't even know you. Why would I be jealous? I'm still discovering myself and where I might fit in. Which means I want to explore. See what my options are."

Marcus didn't seem convinced. "I see. Well, why don't you let me help you explore? I know I came on strong last week, but I promise to be a good boy."

I studied his innocent expression. He seemed sincere,

and there was almost a thread of pleading in his tone. I sighed. "I'll be honest. You make me a little nervous. I don't know if I'm ready for your kind of 'help'. Hell, I don't even know if I'm submissive."

"Sweetness, trust me when I tell you, you're definitely submissive. Look, I'll take it slow. Why don't you come to Eden and see for yourself. You can meet me there, and I'll give you a tour. Introduce you to some people. You can watch a few scenes. And, if you decide you want to play, I'd be happy to accommodate you in any way you'd like."

My brain was telling me no, but my body was screaming yes. This man was making me feel things I'd never felt before. It was slightly unnerving, but also exciting. My sex life was non-existent. What if this was what I'd been waiting for? Someone to guide me. To help me navigate this new environment. I was desperate to feel a connection with someone. Why not this man who seemed clearly interested in me, even if I wasn't sure why.

Before I could stop myself, I blurted out, "Okay, I'll go."

Marcus blinked and his eyes widened in surprise. I was just as shocked by my response. Then he smiled, and my belly fluttered. Lord, he was gorgeous.

"You have no idea how happy this makes me."

He reached out and I placed my hand in his. He brought my knuckles to his lips and pressed a soft kiss on them. I shivered at the heat even after he released his hold.

"Give me your phone number, and I'll text you the address for Eden. Dress however you feel comfortable. Doors open tomorrow night at eight." He pulled his phone out of his pocket.

Still trembling from his touch, I gave him my number.

He keyed it in, and a few seconds later, my phone chirped at an incoming text. I glanced at it to make sure it was from him, then my eyes returned to his.

"I'll be there."

"Good. Now, why don't we go shoot some pool?"

He gave me his elbow, and I only hesitated briefly before threading my arm through his. I followed beside him as we headed to a game already in play. The rest of the night was spent with Marcus trying to teach me how to break. Eventually I relaxed and ended up having the best night. When I finally left, I was more than anxious to see what Eden, and this man, had to offer.

CHAPTER 4

MY PHONE RANG, right as I walked through my front door. The screen read 'Caller Unknown', so I hesitated to answer.

"Hello?"

Static.

"Hello?" I repeated.

I began to lower the phone from my ear to disconnect the call when a guttural voice finally answered.

"Did you enjoy your run, Marcus?"

I stopped the towel mid-swipe across my sweaty face and pulled it away. "Is that you, Evan, you little shit?"

"Tsk. Tsk. That's no way to talk to an old friend," the caller taunted.

"We've never been friends. Now, what the fuck do you want?"

"You know what I want. You have no right to keep her from me."

I paced my kitchen floor, my steps angry. "I want you to listen, and listen well. Grace is somewhere you will never find her. You, on the other hand, will soon be rotting behind bars. Again. Do you understand?"

At first there was silence, then a menacing growl. "You're fucking with the wrong man. I will find that bitch, and when I do, she'll regret ever leaving me. You can't hide her forever. When I find her, I'll make her pay. Do *you* understand?"

"Don't you dare threaten her or me. I will end you, Evan. Make no mistake about it."

Silence was the only reply. "Evan?"

Nothing.

I slammed the phone down on the counter. "Fuck."

Grabbing it again, I quickly keyed in another number.

"Connor Black."

"Evan just called. He, or someone he's paid, is watching me, because he knew I'd just got home from running."

Connor cussed and yelled in the background. When he returned, rage colored his tone. "I'm putting a tracker on your phone in case something happens, and I'm going to start tracing your calls. I need you to come into the office. I'm also going to up the security detail on Grace, and I'm sending one to you."

"No. You can put whatever kind of tracking device you want, but don't waste resources on me. Your primary job is to protect that house. Nothing else matters. Are you listening to me, Connor?"

"Connor?" I repeated when he continued to ignore me.

He exhaled in frustration. "Fine. But I'm going on record that I'm not happy about this. You know as well as I do that nothing is going to stop him from looking for Grace. He's obsessed. And a fucking sociopath."

"Which is why they need more protection."

"And they'll get it," Connor replied firmly.

"Thank you. Give me about an hour and I'll stop by your office."

"I'll make sure Margaret knows you're coming."

"See you soon."

Before disconnecting the call, Connor spoke a final warning. "Watch your back Marcus, and don't take any fucking chances."

I nodded. "Got it. Later."

After hitting the end button, I tossed the phone back on the counter and headed into the bathroom for a quick shower. Worry churned in my belly. Once dressed, I grabbed my keys and phone and headed to my car.

I kept glancing in my rear view mirror, but didn't see signs of anyone following me. Soon, I was pulling into the parking garage attached to the office building that housed Connor's security and protection firm.

The elevator door opened to the fifteenth floor. His assistant, Margaret, was seated behind her desk.

I threw on the charm with a disarming smile when she raised her eyes at my entrance. "You look beautiful this morning, my dear."

She blushed and shooed me with her hand. "Always the flatterer, Marcus."

Margaret was sixty if she was a day.

"What are you doing here on a Saturday? Doesn't that boss of yours ever give you a day off?"

"Of course, I do." Connor stepped out of his office, a scowl on his face, which turned to a genuine smile when he turned to the older woman. "Thank you, Margaret. Now, will you go home?"

"I'm just finishing up this filing and I'll be out of your hair in no time."

He merely shook his head and gestured me into his office, closing the door behind us.

"Hand me your phone."

Used to his brusqueness, I pulled it out of my pocket. While he did whatever it was, I headed over to the fully stocked bar and poured myself a gin and tonic, not caring it was only nine in the morning. I settled onto the love seat next to it and waited. I didn't speak while he worked. Just let him do his job. Once he was done, he tossed the phone back to me and sat at his desk. He placed a pair of reading glasses on and pecked away at his keyboard.

"I put a small chip near your SIM card. It will let us track your phone wherever it goes. I'm also plugging your phone number into a program we use. It will trace every call you receive and every call you make. Which means if Evan calls again, we should be able to triangulate his location."

I took a sip of my drink. "I'll do my best to keep him on the phone if he calls again. I doubt he will though. He wants to keep me guessing. Keep me on edge. He enjoys fucking with me."

Connor finished typing into his computer and set his glasses on his desk before locking gazes with me. "Which is why I'm highly against you not having some form of security."

"Evan is a bully. He's not going to touch me, because he has no power over me. Not physically anyway. Which is what he craves. He only wants to fuck with my head."

"What about this woman you're hot for? Have you thought of her? What if he decides to go after her?"

My breath froze in my chest. "Why would he? She's of no use to him. Besides, we just met. It's not like we've even gone out on a date."

Connor crossed his arms over his chest. "She's coming to Eden tonight, correct? There's obviously something going on between you two."

I shook my head. "There's nothing going on between us. Not really. She's interested in the lifestyle, and I'm, I don't know, mentoring her I guess."

He laughed, but it wasn't amused. "You and I both know you're full of shit."

I rose from the couch, washed and rinsed my now empty glass, and returned it to its place. "I'll see you tonight."

Connor's voice stopped me when I reached the door. "Marcus."

I turned my head to look over my shoulder at him.

"Just think about what I said."

Nodding, I left his office and made my way back home, his warning playing loudly in my head.

CHAPTER 5

I PULLED into the warehouse district and looked around. This was an area of Pinegrove I was definitely not familiar with. Then again, there was no reason for me to be. Most of the businesses here had been shut down, although by the looks of things, there were still a few operating. Several vehicles were parked around a couple of the buildings, but no one milled about. There were no restaurants or flashing club lights to signify which building might be occupied. All seemed quiet and empty.

I kept glancing down at my phone's GPS while it spoke directions to me. I made a couple of turns until it told me I'd reached my destination. I noticed quite a lot of cars in an open parking lot, so I found an empty spot and pulled in. I exited the car and swiveled my head back and forth trying to figure out where the faint, pulsating music was coming from. I followed the direction I thought it generated from and crossed the street to discover it getting slightly louder. I stopped in front of one of the buildings with no windows and pressed my ear against the door. I could feel the vibrations against the side of my face. Before I could stop myself, I pounded on the door and waited.

Within moments, the door opened and my head tilted back and back. My gaze traveled up a skin-tight gray t-shirt that hugged the man's body so tightly his nipples were visible until finally I met his eyes. Their hazel depths twinkled with amusement. I stepped back a fraction and took in the rest of him; Dirty blond hair that touched his shoulders, dark blue jeans, and shit kicker boots. In his ear rested a security earpiece with attached microphone.

"Good evening."

"Um, hi. Is this Club Eden? I'm supposed to be meeting someone, um, Marcus, here." My voice came out raspy and lacked confidence.

"May I tell him who's here?" the giant asked politely.

"Penny."

He pressed a button on the bluetooth and spoke to whomever was on the other end.

"Can you let Mr. Allen know there's a Penny here to see him?"

The man's attention returned to me. "Come on in. He'll be right out. I'm Philip."

I smiled nervously. "Oh, hi, I'm Penny. Duh, of course it is, I just told you that. Um… anyway. Thanks."

He opened the door wide enough for me to pass by him. I startled when it slammed closed behind us. He merely smiled when I glanced at him. While I waited, my eyes scanned the small room we stood in. To the naked eye, it appeared lackluster.

Bare white walls surrounded us, void of any pictures or paintings. Semi-translucent wall sconces with pale yellow bulbs were the only decoration. Immediately to the left of the door we'd entered was a coat closet. Next to the closet was a large, wooden desk with intricate scrollwork along the border.

It seemed like an interesting piece of furniture so I moved to get a closer look. I had to squint to make out the designs. My eyes widened in shock, and I jumped back like I'd been burned, when I realized what I'd been seeing. Thanks to my fair skin, my face felt hot with a flush of embarrassment, and oddly, arousal. The intricate carving along the edges of the desk showed men and women in different sexual positions. The attention to detail was incredible, displaying every dip, curve, and crevice of the people etched into the wood.

"See anything that interests you?"

I yelped in surprise at the deep voice behind me. I turned to find Marcus standing next to Philip, both of them attempting to conceal their laughter.

"I was just admiring the… workmanship." My stupid blush continued to spread, and I could feel my chest getting hotter.

He smiled with genuine amusement. "I see that. If you're done admiring, are you ready to go inside?"

Hell no I wasn't ready. Instead, I lied, with a shaky smile. "Of course."

Marcus ushered me through a doorway hidden in the wall opposite the coat closet and scandalous desk. I kept silent during our walk down the hall toward the growing loudness of the music. As we turned a corner, the hallway opened up into a vast room filled with people. The lights were dim and cast a purplish glow around the room, illuminating it enough to make out the various people throughout the place.

What the hell had I gotten myself into?

Red couches and lounge chairs were scattered around, including a large cluster tucked inside an alcove immediately to the right of the doorway. They were filled with men and women wearing varying amounts of clothing, including nothing at all, engaged in everything that ranged from casual conversation to different sex acts.

One woman knelt at a man's feet, giving him a blow job. Around her neck was a collar with an attached leash, which disappeared inside the man's fisted grasp. There was a young man sitting silently at the feet of a tiny blonde woman wearing blue glasses and dressed in a blue satin corset and boy shorts. His head rested on her lap as she lovingly stroked his hair while she conversed with another woman in a chair next to them.

My eyes rounded like saucers and my mouth dropped open farther as I continued to scan the club. Immediately opposite us, people were observing a suspension demonstration. I'd seen various ropework and suspensions during my research, and the artistry of it always had me amazed. And turned on. I'd imaged being naked and wrapped in an intricate design with rope between my legs, decorating my back, belly, and breasts as I seemingly floated in space.

To the left of the doorway in which we stood were four or five alcoves built into the wall with curtains tied open. People hovered outside each one, observing the different activities and demonstrations going on inside. My fascination belonged to the scene to the right of all the various alcoves. Along the perpendicular wall, a built-up stage rose from the floor where a shirtless man expertly flogged a naked female tied to a St. Andrew's Cross. Even from this distance, it was obvious the sub was thoroughly enjoying it. Wetness glistened on the inside of her thighs, and her nipples were ruched from excitement. Her back and ass were red from the flogger's tails, and the sound of the falls echoed through the room, along with her cries of pleasure. In my dreams, my arms and legs were bound to that cross, my ass naked and on display for all to see. I waited in anticipation for each thwap of the flogger. My nipples puckered, and my breathing sped up. I became so lost in the show I didn't realize Marcus had guided me off to the side of the stage and into the shadows until he murmured in my ear.

"Do you like what you see?" His hot breath sent a shiver down my spine.

"Yes." My voice came out breathy.

"I'm glad you're enjoying the show."

I thought I felt a ghost of a touch, his lips against my skin, but it didn't happen again, so I must have been mistaken. My heart raced at the thought. I wanted Marcus to touch me.

He continued speaking, his voice low and coaxing. "Can you see her pushing back into each strike? She wants what he is giving her. She *needs* what he is giving her. It's his job to provide her with the things she needs. She knows this makes him happy, and she wants to please him. To submit to him."

I unconsciously pressed my thighs together to try and quell the ache between them. My pussy was slick with wetness under my dress and my clit throbbed with the need to be touched.

"Are you imagining that you're the one up there while

everyone watches? Watching as your back and ass turn a bright red from each strike?" Marcus growled.

"Yes, Sir," I choked out, the honorific slipping out without intent. I wanted to come so bad, and I could feel myself right on the edge. My eyes drifted shut as I tried to focus on the sensations and chase the elusive orgasm.

"Don't close your eyes," he barked. "Keep watching the stage."

My eyes flew open at his command. I listened to what he'd told me and forced my attention back on to the stage as we watched the scene continue to unfold. The flogging had stopped, and the Dom now squatted behind the bound woman, his hands squeezing her ass cheeks while he devoured her from behind. The sub writhed when the Dom moved one hand from her hip and plunged his fingers inside her pussy, his mouth not moving from her ass. I squirmed and moaned with arousal.

My gaze remained fixated on the couple, when suddenly, in concert with each other, both the onstage sub and I found our release. Pleasure burst through me and shudders coursed down my body, causing my knees to buckle. Strong arms wrapped around my waist and pulled me against a hard chest. Without Marcus' support, I would have collapsed in a heap on the floor. He hadn't even been touching me and I'd come. Mortification spread through my body.

"Oh my god. Oh my god," I repeated and covered my face in shame. "I can't believe that just happened."

Marcus reached for me, and without much resistance, I let him draw me into his arms, where he began stroking my hair.

"You have nothing to be ashamed of. Now, come with me and let's get you something to drink."

He took my hand and led me to a couch tucked away in a corner. I sagged against him once we were seated. He wrapped an arm around me and pulled me closer. I rested my head against his shoulder. Neither of us spoke as he lightly kissed the top of my head and stroked my hair away from my face. I forgot all about my earlier embarrassment. I'd never felt more at peace.

CHAPTER 6

WITH PENNY RESTING AGAINST ME, I motioned for one of the dungeon monitors, or DM, to bring me a bottle of water. Several minutes later, he reappeared, unscrewed the cap, and handed it to me. I nodded my thanks and tapped Penny's arm.

"Here, I want you to drink this."

I reluctantly released my hold on her when she sat up. I could have held her all night.

"Thank you." She took the bottle from me and swallowed down several sips. I closed my hand around it when she tried to hand it back.

"No, I want you to drink all of it. You need the hydration."

"Yes, sir." We both froze at the term, even though it wasn't meant the way it came out.

Penny nervously glanced around while she continued drinking. I studied her while she observed the main floor of Eden.

I looked out and tried to picture it from a newcomer's

eyes. It was difficult considering I'd been in the lifestyle for over twenty years. When I glanced back at her, our eyes met and the sexual tension between us crackled. My fingertips burned with the need to touch her.

"It's exciting watching others, isn't it?" My voice was soft and coaxing. I almost groaned when she licked her lips.

"I never realized," she whispered in awe.

"Come on, let's explore."

Without giving her a chance to reply, I stood and pulled her to her feet refusing to loosen my grasp on her even after she came to standing. Hand in hand we walked around the room, stopping first at the alcoves located near the door that we'd bypassed earlier. I was curious to see her reaction to them since each one housed a different kink. We stopped at the first curtained-off space where a completely naked woman laid spread eagle on her back on a massage table. Her wrists and ankles were bound in rope that was tied to the legs of the table.

"Watch what he does," I murmured to Penny so I didn't interrupt the couple's scene.

A man stood next to the bound woman with a violet wand in his hand and ran it across her breasts. I wondered if Penny noticed the slight sing of the electrical current running through the wand. The woman cried for more.

"Does it hurt?" Penny kept her voice quiet, but I could hear the excitement behind her question.

"Only in the best of ways."

With the wand singing a little louder, the man moved it from her breasts to her crotch. The bound sub arched her back off the table and cried out when he reached his destination. The pleasure radiating off her was tangible, and I could see Penny shiver in response.

I gave her hand a gentle tug. "Let's keep moving."

In the next cordoned off area was a fire cupping demonstration.

Her eyes widened in wonder. "What is that?"

While the Dom swabbed the inside of glass cups, varying in size from a shot glass to a rocks glass, with ethyl alcohol I explained how the process worked. I saw the fascination in Penny's expression when he lit the alcohol inside on fire and placed the cups top down in random spots along the woman's back.

"I know we really haven't talked about this yet tonight, but are you still unsure whether you're submissive or not?" I couldn't help but ask. "Especially after all you've just experienced."

She appeared embarrassed if the sudden flush across her chest was any indication. Her gaze darted to me and back to the scene and back to me again. She straightened her shoulders confidently.

"I think you were right at the munch last week."

Penny turned back to continue observing the couple without another word, and I couldn't help but feel a sense of self-satisfaction. Based on her comment, she agreed with my assessment. She was most definitely submissive. Instinct told me she'd also been researching the lifestyle since we last met. I tested my theory.

"Have you come up with a list of soft and hard limits yet?"

She flushed and continued avoiding eye contact with me. "Maybe a few."

I held back a smile. "Would you like to add this to your

list of soft limits?"

Her nod was barely discernible, but I saw it anyway.

"Why don't we head to the bar?"

I took the opportunity to touch her again. With my hand on the small of her back, I led Penny away from the nearly complete scene. I helped her onto a stool, leaving my hand where it was. I gestured to the bartender.

While we waited for his arrival, I made small talk. "Have you enjoyed your evening?"

"I have actually. I wasn't sure what to expect." She pivoted slightly toward me, my hand gliding off her with the movement.

"I'm glad. I'd really enjoy getting to know you more."

"I'd like that. A lot." She smiled and I brushed Penny's hair back from her forehead. I slowly leaned down, stopping right before our lips met. When she didn't offer a protest, I brushed my mouth across hers gently in a teasing move. Her tongue darted out to wet her lips and tickled mine. It was all I needed to deepen the kiss. I coaxed her mouth open and soon our tongues were dueling for control. I nipped her bottom lip reminding her who was in charge. She whimpered in response and I took over.

The kiss went on for minutes and the room around us faded. She tasted like a combination of strawberries and cream. I fisted her hair and devoured her a little longer, before finally pulling back to gasp in air. Penny was just as short of breath. I rested my forehead on hers as our breathing settled back into a normal pattern.

A whistle of appreciation sounded in my ear. Penny quickly pulled away, and I turned to glare at the intruder. Internally I groaned.

"Good evening, Marcus. Miss," a friend, and part owner of Eden, greeted us with a charming smile.

"Donovan," I bit out in annoyance.

He ignored my obvious irritation and merely smiled brighter. "Why don't you introduce me to your lovely lady friend?"

Knowing he wasn't going anyway, I made the introduction. "Penny, this is my friend, and fellow Dom, Donovan Jeffries."

He reached out to clasp her hand and brought it to his lips dusting a light kiss across her knuckles, never taking his eyes off her.

"A pleasure," he drawled in the seductive tone he liked to use. It had never bothered me before, but I bristled when he used it on Penny. "Tell me, what is a beautiful young woman like yourself doing with an ugly old man like Marcus here?"

Donovan continued to hold her hand, caressing her knuckles with his thumb. I wanted to rip him away from her, but I merely clenched my fists at my side. Penny blushed at the attention he was giving her, which didn't surprise me. He was a charmer and most women soaked it up. Despite her obvious pleasure at his compliment, she gently pulled her hand from his grasp.

"We're on a date."

I almost laughed at her response. I wouldn't call this a date exactly, but I wasn't going to argue with her.

Donovan glanced over at me with a cheeky grin. "Lucky you. You have great taste in submissives, Marcus. Perhaps the three of us can get better acquainted later."

"Perhaps."

"Well, you know where to find me if you decide you're interested." He winked at Penny before leaving us alone.

I turned to see her staring at me. "Did he mean what I think he meant?"

I merely smiled, letting her come to her own conclusion.

"I see," she sputtered.

I took pity on her. "Don't worry, Donovan is a harmless flirt. He's also a respectful Dom, believe it or not, and would never push you to do anything you weren't interested in."

Penny stared at me for a moment, assessing. "And what about you?"

I returned her look with a puzzled one of my own. "What about me?"

"Would you push me to do something I wasn't interested in?"

"No fucking way."

Penny took my hand. "I believe you."

I sagged in relief and gripped her hand. "Thank you."

We didn't speak for several more minutes. I cleared my throat.

"I'd love to see you again. What about dinner tomorrow night?"

She nodded. "I'd like that."

"Great. Why don't we say six-thirty. I'll pick you up."

We spent the next several hours talking and getting to know each other better. When it was time to go I walked her to her car. With a too-brief kiss, I said my goodbyes and told her I'd call her in the morning. I strode over to my car, never noticing the man sitting inside the parked car at the end of the road, observing us.

CHAPTER 7

I HAD no idea what I was going to wear tonight. It was such a ridiculous problem to worry about, but sudden anxiety filled me. It had been five years since I'd been out on a real date. Ever since I'd broken up with my ex-boyfriend. The one who'd practically destroyed my self-worth.

Over the last couple years I'd fought back against the insecurities that had become so engrained in me during my relationship with Troy. I hadn't fully recovered my confidence or self-esteem, but every day was better than the last. Today, though, was bad. I panicked. I had a few close girlfriends, but if I told them I was going on a date, there were going to be so many questions I wasn't ready to answer. It wasn't like I thought they'd disapprove of Marcus or how we'd met, but it was still awkward and way too early to drop something like this on them.

Not knowing what else to do, I grabbed my phone and scanned my contacts for Bridget's number.

"Hello?"

"Hey, Bridget. It's Penny, from the munch. I'm sorry to call you so early, but do you have a minute?"

"Okay, what's up? You sound desperate."

I almost laughed at how quickly she pegged it. "It's silly, really, but I didn't know who else to call. I'm going out on a date with Marcus tonight, and I don't know what to wear."

Now that I said it out loud, I realized how dumb I sounded. There was no turning back now though. I'd already made the call.

"Babe, you called the right person. Do you know where *Unique Boutique* is on Campbell Street?" Bridget's calm demeanor helped me a little.

"Isn't that the fancy clothing boutique in downtown? I'm pretty sure that's out of my price range." I'd never been there, but I'd heard it was the next up-and-coming business in Pinegrove.

"Just get your ass here."

Damn, for a submissive, she was awfully bossy.

I huffed. "Fine."

"Can you be there in fifteen to twenty minutes?"

I knew the general area I was headed and it was doable. "Yes."

"Perfect. I'll see you then."

Less than fifteen minutes later I was parking on the street in front of the store. The clothes in the window were absolutely adorable, but I still had my reservations about being here for several reasons. One was my budget. I made a great living as a nurse, but I always balked at splurging on myself. Especially on clothes. Mostly, because I hated clothes shopping. I could never find anything that fit right. Which was my other reservation.

I'd never in my life been in a boutique store that carried clothes for women my size.

I peered through the door, but it didn't look like anyone was inside or that any lights were even on. Maybe I was at the wrong place. I knocked on the window and waited. I gave up and headed back to my car. I hadn't taken two steps when a woman yelled out.

"I'm coming. Damn, you got here fast."

I pivoted and saw Bridget briskly walking toward me. She pulled out a set of keys from her purse and unlocked the door to the store.

"Do you work here?" I followed her inside.

She smiled, her eyes sparkling. "Honey, I own this place."

My eyes widened in wonder as I looked around at all the beautiful clothes on display. "Oh wow. I had no idea."

I reached out for a dress that caught my eye and pulled it off the rack. It was stunning. Vintage design. Something I'd love to wear, but had never had the courage. I put it back.

"Come on, let me show you some things." Bridget waved at me to follow her.

"Take a look in this section and see if you find something you like."

Eying her hesitantly, I pulled out a dress at random and looked at the size. My jaw almost dropped. I looked at the tag on another dress and another. Each and every one I looked at was near my size. I glanced over at Bridget who stood with arms crossed and a smug expression on face.

"I carry clothes in almost every size, because I want to serve the entire population of Pinegrove, not just a small segment. I know how difficult it can be to find fashionable clothes, especially at a reasonable price. I love clothes. They're my life, and I want others to get some joy out of them as well."

I continued browsing in awe and utter excitement. "This makes me so happy. Thank you."

Four dresses later, I headed into the dressing room to try them on. I modeled each one for her. She pinned and tucked a few things and eventually I settled on a shimmery eggplant colored wrap dress that hit just above my knees. I felt beautiful in it. Scared, I lifted the price tag, and blinked. That couldn't be right.

"Bridget, I think there's a mistake on the price." I stepped out of the dressing room holding the dress and tag out to her.

She looked down at it and shook her head. "No, that's correct."

"Are you sure?"

"Come on, I'll ring you up."

After far less pounding to my pocketbook than I thought, I was now the proud owner of a stunning new dress. My anxiety about tonight suddenly calmed.

"So, where is Marcus taking you?" Bridget handed me the bag with its cute tissue paper sticking out.

"I have no idea. He just said dinner."

"Have you been to Eden yet?"

My face heated. "Last night actually."

She squealed in excitement. "And? Did you and Marcus play?"

"No. We just watched some scenes and talked. Although, I did get propositioned for a threesome by one of Marcus' friends."

Bridget laughed. "Donovan?"

"Yes! How did you know?"

She merely rolled her eyes. "I think Donovan does that to every new female visitor to Eden. Honestly, I think it's nothing but a shock tactic. To see what kind of reaction he gets. He's harmless. Just a giant flirt. I don't think I've ever met a more charming Dom. I've never scened with him, but I've been around long enough to know he's a genuinely nice guy."

"That's what Marcus said too. About him being a harmless flirt. But anyway, back to my date. "I don't think I remember how to act on one,it's been so long."

"Be yourself. Nothing more to it than that. You talk and laugh and hopefully have a good time." She shrugged.

"I just feel like there are so many more expectations to this. I mean all I think about when I'm with Marcus is sex."

"Well, I hope so," Bridget cackled.

I glared back. "Good god, not like that. I mean I'm going on a date with a man who's a Dominant. One I met at a munch and then hung out with at a kink club. It feels like more than just a dinner date."

Bridget took my shopping bag and set it on the counter. Then she clasped my hands in hers. "I know you're new to this, but I'm going to impart some great knowledge on you here. Are you listening?"

She waited until I nodded before she continued. "Marcus is only a Dom because you grant him your submission. That's how the whole power exchange works. In reality, you're the one with the power. You trusting Marcus transfers that power to him. You have a safe word. If and when you use it, Marcus releases the power you've given him and returns it to you. If this is only dinner and nothing more, then that's fine. If it becomes something more, remember you are in charge."

I tried wrapping my head around Bridget's advice. In a weird, convoluted way, it made sense. Our date could be nothing more than dinner. It was up to me to decide if I wanted more. With that realization, I felt an intense relief course through me.

Tonight could be whatever I wanted it to be.

My shoulders sagged like a weight had been taken off them. "Thank you. I feel infinitely better now."

She released my hands with a soft squeeze and handed me back my bag. "Good, now go get ready and have an amazing time."

I waved goodbye and headed home, excitement buzzing through me at seeing Marcus tonight.

CHAPTER 8

I WOKE to another threatening letter. Connor's warning rang in my head, but I truly didn't think Evan would have any interest in Penny. It was just a date, nothing more.

Now, I stood in front of her house. I knocked on the door and while I waited, my eyes scanned the street around me watching for anything that seemed "off".

When it opened, I stood speechless. She was breathtaking.

She greeted me with a simple "Hi."

In that moment, I realized what a mistake this could be.

She cleared her throat in the uncomfortable silence and took a small step backward opening the door further. "Would you like to come in?"

I hesitated briefly, but then stepped past her. "Thank you."

I wandered around her living room, pausing here and there to examine pictures scattered around. Most were pictures of her with friends, but there were also a few with a couple who I assumed were her parents.

"If this is how you treat women you ask out on a date, I think we should call it a night before it even begins. You've only spoken two words to me in the five minutes you've been here. Submissive or not, I'm certainly no doormat. I think it would be best if you left."

I slowly pivoted in Penny's direction. She stood with hands on hips, lips pressed tightly together, her eyes narrowed in irritation. I'd never seen a more beautiful woman.

"You're right. I've been an asshole. I apologize for ignoring you. I swear it wasn't my intent. Honestly, my thoughts were elsewhere and that was rude of me. I'm sorry."

Her indignation deflated at my words and her features softened. "I'm sorry for practically biting your head off."

I closed the distance between us and cupped her jaw, my thumb brushing across her cheek, needing to feel her skin beneath mine. I groaned when she leaned slightly into my touch.

"Don't apologize. You deserve to be treated with respect." I reached down and threaded my fingers through hers. "Are you ready?"

"I'm ready."

She grabbed her purse from the end table and we headed out to my vehicle. I opened the door for her and once she was settled, I closed it. I slid in behind the wheel and sent her wink and smile.

"Buckle up," I warned her as we set off.

An hour later we were enjoying a delicious dinner at a local favorite, The Windmill.

"So, if I remember correctly, you're a trauma nurse?"

Penny set her fork down. "I am. I've been working in the E.D. for the last six years."

"I imagine that's quite the demanding job. One that's often thankless I'm sure."

She rested her hands on the table. "It is on both accounts. But, it's also a rewarding and fulfilling career. I've worked in both private practice and trauma. Each has its benefits, of course. I found that the benefits of working in trauma outweigh those in a general practice office. I love the fast-paced nature and the adrenaline rush from it."

"Ah, an adrenaline junkie, huh?" I asked with a smile.

She laughed a little. "Only when it comes to my work. Otherwise, not so much. What about you? I don't think you've ever told me what you do."

"That's because what I do is very boring," I said drily. "Financial advising is yawn-inducing. I promise, crunching numbers is nothing to get excited over."

"But do you enjoy it?"

I paused for a moment. I don't think anyone had ever asked me that. "Yes, actually, I like my job."

"Then that's all that matters," she said matter-of-factly. "Can I ask you another question?"

"Of course."

This time, she briefly hesitated before leaning a little closer and lowering her voice. "How did you get into the lifestyle?"

I sat back in my chair. "My college girlfriend and I experimented with kink. It snowballed from there."

"Wow, that's a long time."

"When—" my next word froze in my throat.

I jumped out of my seat fast enough to tip the chair backwards and took off at a clip across the restaurant. I could hear Penny yelling my name, but I didn't stop. I dodged bodies as I raced to catch the son of bitch I'd seen across the room. Throwing the front door open, I came to an abrupt halt. Nothing. He'd disappeared.

"God damn it," I screamed out in fury causing multiple people walking down the sidewalk to turn and gape at me.

"Marcus?" Penny's hesitant voice came from behind me. "What's going on?"

Ignoring her, I continued scanning the area. There was no sign of him. *Fuck.*

"C'mon, I'm taking you home."

Throughout the ride back to her house, she remained silent. All I did was clench and unclench my fists around the steering wheel, trying to rein in my rage. And fear. I was pissed off. Not only at Evan Banks, but at myself. Connor had been right. It wasn't fair to Penny to drag her into this bullshit. Evan wasn't playing by anyone's rules but his own, which meant it was up to me to protect her. That meant leaving her alone. Pulling into her driveway, I put the car in park and turned toward her.

"I don't think this is going to work out between us. I'm sorry."

She blinked and blinked again. Then she drew her shoulders back and held her head high. "I see."

When she reached for the door handle her hand trembled.

"Let me walk you to your door."

Her head whipped back in my direction and she spoke

through clenched teeth. "I'm fine, thank you. Enjoy the rest of your evening, Marcus."

Before I could argue further, she slammed the door and hurried up the walkway. I remained sitting there long after she'd gone inside.

CHAPTER 9

IT HAD BEEN two days since Marcus… broke up with me, I guess? Although we hadn't even really been dating. Bridget had texted, but I'd blown her off. There really wasn't much *to* say. Honestly, I hadn't wanted to talk about it anyway. What I wanted to do was forget about this whole submissive thing and move on with my life. I didn't think the lifestyle was for me. Today, I planned on enjoying my day off. I'd come into my favorite local coffee shop with my book, and I'd been sitting in one of the big comfy chairs in the corner sipping an iced coffee while I read. Except I wasn't reading. I sat there, my thoughts drifting to the last two weeks and wondering what happened to suddenly change Marcus' mind.

"Excuse me, miss."

I looked up to see a good-looking, sandy-blond. He was staring directly at me with a puzzled expression on his face.

"I'm sorry, were you talking to me?"

He smiled, although I noticed it didn't quite reach his

eyes. "I don't mean to bother you, and this is going to sound awful, but you look really familiar to me. I just can't place your name. Have we met before?"

I studied him, but I couldn't place his face. "No, sorry, I don't think so."

He grinned sheepishly. "I know that sounded like a corny pick up line, and I promise I didn't mean it that way. I just swear I've seen your beautiful face somewhere. I'm Evan by the way."

I blushed slightly as I shook the hand he offered. "Penny."

"Wow, with your hair color, it fits you perfectly. Of course, I'd expect nothing less from a gorgeous woman such as yourself. I bet your boyfriend tells you all the time how stunning you are."

At first, I was flattered. Then the cynical part of me wondered what his angle was. The longer he stared at me, the more wary I grew. Women's intuition was telling me I needed to leave. I decided to trust my instinct.

I took the last swallow of my coffee and picked up my purse. I tossed my book in it and rose from my seat.

"I didn't mean to make you uncomfortable." Evan made to stand up.

I waved him back to his seat. "You didn't. Enjoy your day."

I hurried toward the door, and just as I reached it, I heard him call out to me. "Hey, Penny."

I paused with my hand on the glass and looked over my shoulder.

His smile was gone and there was this glower of menace on his face now. "Tell Marcus that Evan sends his regards."

I suppressed the shiver that ran over me and pushed the door open, disappearing outside. I rushed toward my car and once I was behind the wheel I glanced in my rearview mirror. Evan had exited the coffee shop and now stood in the middle of the sidewalk watching me. A chill crept up my spine and gooseflesh covered my arms. I cranked the key in the ignition and quickly sped away, my eyes barely leaving the mirror the entire drive home. I pulled into my garage and quickly shut the door. Then, I hustled inside and paranoia made me check all my window and door locks.

Sitting on the edge of the couch, I wrapped my arms around my body and tried to warm the sudden coldness rushing through me. Evan had made me nervous, and I didn't know why. I only knew his message creeped me out. I needed to tell someone, but I didn't want to talk to Marcus. That left Bridget. I rose and grabbed my phone out of my purse and sent her a quick text. Moments later she responded.

Bridget: What's going on with you and Marcus?

Me: Too much to say over text. Are you busy?

B: No. Call me.

She answered on the first ring. "Okay, what the hell is going on?"

"Do you know a guy by the name of Evan?"

"Mother fucker. Are you all right?" Her words were rushed and full of worry. Nervousness rose inside me again.

"Yes, I'm fine. Bridget, who is he?"

"You really need to talk to Marcus. And Connor."

"Marcus and I are no longer speaking. Who's Connor?"

"Connor owns Black Light Security."

My stomach heaved. My voice trembled. "Do you have Connor's number?"

There was rustling in the background. "I'm looking for it. Hold on. Are you in a safe place?"

While she was finding his number, I walked into the kitchen for a pen and paper. "Yes, I'm home. He was at the coffee shop while I was there. He was still standing outside when I took off. I don't think he followed me. I was watching."

"Okay, you ready?"

"Go ahead."

I wrote down the number she rattled off. "I'm going to call him now."

"Call me back as soon as you get off the phone with him," she ordered.

"I will. Thanks, Bridget."

As soon as I disconnected our call, I dialed Connor.

I tapped my foot impatiently while I waited for him to answer.

"Black." His voice was brusque.

"Is this Connor?"

"Speaking. Who is this?"

"My name is Penny Stephens. Bridget from Eden told me to call you. I think I need your help."

CHAPTER 10

Meet me at your sub's house. Now.

THAT WAS ALL the text I'd just received from Connor said. The only person he could be talking about was Penny. But she wasn't my sub. Not now. Maybe not ever. Especially after the other night. I knew how hurt she'd been when she'd lashed out at me. I didn't blame her. I'd been an asshole. It didn't matter though. I did what needed to be done to protect her. Which is what now had me worried with the message on my phone. And why I was in my car on the way to her house.

When I turned onto her street, my gut clenched when I spotted Connor's SUV in the driveway. *Fuck.* I parked on the street and almost ran up the sidewalk. I didn't even have to knock. The door swung open and he stepped back to let me enter. My vision immediately homed in on Penny's pale face as she sat huddled in the corner of her couch, her feet tucked underneath her. I rushed over to her, not caring if she wanted me there or not. I crouched down in front of her and reached out to palm her cheek.

"Are you okay?" I asked with gravel in my throat.

She leaned into my touch and placed her hand over mine. "I'm fine now. Just a little shook up."

I pivoted a little and glared up at Connor who'd moved into the middle of the room.

"What the fuck is going on?"

He tilted his chin in Penny's direction. "Evan made an introduction earlier today while she was out having coffee. He sends his regards."

I abruptly stood and rounded on Connor. "Are you fucking kidding me? You're telling me that he just casually walked into a store and was within ten feet of her?"

Connor's face was rigid with tension. "It would appear so."

"Goddamn it." I pounded my fist on my leg in rage. "She needs protection."

He acknowledged my unspoken order. "Already working on it."

"Marcus."

Penny rose to her feet and stood there looking scared and uncertain.

"I need you to tell me who Evan is."

I stepped over to her and ran my hands down her arms, grasping her fingers. "Come, sit."

She took her previous position on the couch and I sat next to her, her hands still held in mine.

"Do you remember me mentioning my college girlfriend? The one who I explored kink with?"

"Yes."

"After we broke up, Grace dropped out of school and

went back to her hometown. I didn't see her again until seven years ago."

I paused as I recalled how much she'd changed. How hollow and terrified she was. I swallowed and continued. "Anyway, she told me that after she returned home, she ended up marrying the son of one of the men who worked for her father. Soon after the wedding, her husband changed. At first, it was verbal abuse. Then it escalated to physical abuse. She lived in fear for her life for ten years. She wanted out, but didn't know how to get help. I was the only person she thought to turn to. You remember Donovan?"

Penny nodded.

"He works for the Assistant District Attorney's office. He's extremely familiar with several battered women's shelters through his work there, so I put her in touch with him to get the help she needed and to file for divorce from her husband. Needless to say, when the divorce papers were delivered, he went ballistic. Tracked her down, beat the shit out of, and almost killed her. He was sent to prison. Well, now he's out, and he wants Grace back."

Penny sharply inhaled. "Evan is Grace's ex-husband, isn't he? Somehow he's connected me to you and today's little introduction was his way of letting you know it."

It wasn't a question, but I answered anyway. "Yes."

She pulled her hands from mine, then rose from the couch and began to pace. She walked back and forth across the room before pivoting to face us. "So, what happens next?"

I hated that she'd severed our connection and the flat tone in her question. Connor chose that moment to speak up. I'd completely forgotten he was here, my entire focus had been on this woman.

"You get round-the-clock security or you go to a safe house. Your choice."

Her laugh was hollow. "Neither of those are the greatest choices."

Connor raised and lowered a single shoulder. "No, but those are the only two you have."

"Well, a safe house is out of the question. I have a job. Bills to pay. I can't just disappear."

"Then it's a twenty-four-seven protective detail. They'll be stationed outside your house as well as at your place of employment. You don't go anywhere without them."

I spoke up while I rose from my seated position. "It's for the best, Penny."

Her hands went to her hips. "Best for who, Marcus? Best for Grace? For me? For you?"

Damn, I shouldn't be turned on by her ferocity, but I was. It was also like she was challenging my Dominant side, and she didn't even know it. It was time she learned.

I prowled toward her, my gaze burning into hers. She lost some of her defiance the closer I got. For every forward step I took, she took one backward, until her back hit the wall. I reached out and threaded my fingers through her hair. I fisted the auburn strands and firmly tugged her head back, forcing her to look up at me. She bit her lip in a nervous gesture.

"It was never my intent for you to get involved in my mess, but now that you are, we're going to come to an understanding. You will accept the protective detail that Connor provides and you won't take any unnecessary chances. Evan doesn't care about you. Hell, he doesn't even care about me. He's obsessed with Grace. Which means he'll keep fucking with me until he finds her. Now, I'm sorry that you've got caught up in all this, but until he's caught I want you safe. Do you understand?"

"Yes, sir," she whispered.

"Good." I dropped a kiss on her forehead and released my hold on her. I turned to Connor. "Do whatever you have to do to keep them out of his reach."

He saluted. "You got it."

CHAPTER 11

IT HAD BEEN three days since the incident with Evan at *A Whole Latte.* As promised, I had twenty-four hour security. When I went to work, someone was with me. Grocery store, same. Yoga, still there. I was starting to learn to ignore their presence, although I didn't think I'd get used to it. In fact, I hoped I didn't. This wasn't what I wanted for my life. I wanted all this to be over and done with. Connor had escorted me to the police station the day after to file a restraining order. It was merely a formality, and nothing but a piece of paper, but it was documentation in case something else happened. I was still pretty pissed that I got dragged into this situation, but since there was nothing I could do about it at the moment, I made do.

Bridget had called multiple times to check in and tell me how sorry she was. I was shocked to discover that she had a hand in helping Marcus' ex, Grace, after Evan had put her in the hospital. Bridget and Donovan had worked together to keep her safe. Grace even stayed with her for a while after Evan was sent to prison. Before she was placed in a safe house, where she remained to this day.

As for Marcus and me, our relationship changed. He'd explained about spotting Evan at dinner the other night and it had terrified him. He hadn't wanted to risk my safety and that was why he'd so abruptly called off us going any further. But since I was now on Evan's radar, Marcus figured it wasn't going to make matters worse if we were seen together. We hadn't gone out on another date yet, but he'd called me every night . I didn't want to admit I was sitting here waiting for his call, even if I was. When he'd gone all Dom on me, something clicked inside. In fact, I was ready to head back to Eden. I refused to let some psychopath keep me from doing the things I wanted to do.

I definitely wasn't ready for public play yet, but I knew there were some private rooms at the back of the club. This whole adventure began because I wanted to explore some unknown part of me. Well, now that I'd discovered this apparent submissive side, it was like a whole new world had opened up. And I'd be damned if I was going to hold back a part of myself now.

Just then my phone rang. I glanced at the clock. Marcus was nothing if not consistent.

"Hi."

"Good evening, Sweetness. How was your day?"

At the sound of his voice, I sank further into the couch cushion, pulling my leg under me to get comfortable.

"Busier than usual. The coming full moon brings out the crazy in people, I swear. We had a stabbing victim and a man who'd been shot twice by his disgruntled neighbor over a stupid tree and property lines. There were also several car accidents. Needless to say, I didn't get to sit down all day, let alone eat. I ended up grabbing a salad and some soup from the grocery store deli on the my way home."

"That's not enough food for you to eat. You better have at least eaten breakfast before you headed in." I picked out the underlying command in there.

"I usually eat a bowl of oatmeal or a couple hard boiled eggs and two pieces of bacon," I defended myself. Regardless of my size, I wasn't much of an eater. I was used to only eating two meals a day due to my work. It wasn't always like today, but when it was, you made it through the day as best you could.

I could almost feel his frown through the phone, so I quickly changed the topic.

"I talked to Bridget yesterday."

There was a huff of air over the line. "We're not done talking about this yet, but I'll let you get away with it for now. So, tell me what Bridget had to say."

"She was telling me about a seven deadly sins masquerade being held at Eden this weekend." Now that I brought it up, I was nervous about the topic.

When I paused too long, Marcus filled in the silence. "I assume you two made plans to attend?"

Bolstering myself with confidence I sat up a little straighter. "Actually, yes. I was wondering if you were going to be there."

"Sweetness, if you're there, so am I. If I remember correctly, you agreed to me helping you. I sure hope you're not going back on your word," he said, his voice full of steel.

"No, sir."

"My god, do you have any idea what it does to me to hear that word coming from your lips? My cock instantly hardens."

"I guess I'll have to say it more often then."

"Oh, you most definitely will." I shivered when his voice dropped an octave and sent a rumble through my belly. I practically melted into a puddle on my sofa.

"If you plan on returning to Eden, I hope you've made a list of soft and hard limits. And that you have a safe word picked out. I know the flogger turned you on, which, by the way, I can't wait to use. I've been itching to redden that ass of yours for weeks now. Speaking of asses, I'd also love to see a plug stretch yours. Then I want to watch my cock thrust in and out of that tight hole. Does the thought of me inside your ass make your pussy wet, Sweetness?"

And just like that, my plan backfired. I whimpered and clenched my thighs together to try and ease the ache now inside me at the picture Marcus painted.

"I'm waiting on an answer, Penny," he growled.

"Yes, Sir."

"Good girl. Now, your soft and hard limits, please."

I preened at the praise. Instantly my mind filled with all the things I wanted to experience at least once. With nothing to do, but forge ahead, I listed them. "I'd like to see how nipple clamps feel. And yes to the flogger, please. I've also wondered what a paddle, or erotic spanking, would feel like. Um, anal sex is also a soft limit. I was really intrigued by that wand thing-y and the fire in the cups too."

Marcus chuckled. "That 'wand thing-y' is a violet wand and it's fire cupping, Sweet."

I blew him a raspberry over the phone. "You knew what I meant."

"I did. I think that's a reasonable list to start with. Now, what about hard limits?"

I thought about some of the kinks I'd learned about during my research. I knew there were probably so many more than the few I'd read about, but a few jumped out at me that I was pretty sure weren't my kink.

"Even being a nurse, I don't think I could handle blood. No peeing and definitely no excrement. I'm also pretty sure I'm not into humiliation. Or a significant amount of pain."

Marcus made a noise I took as acceptance. "I'm not a sadist, so I have no desire to cause you large amounts of pain, but you have to realize that pain and pleasure co-exist almost on the same plane. When you experience pain, it only makes the pleasure that much sweeter, much more intense. For me, though, it's about the power exchange between a Dom and his submissive. You give me power by submitting to me and obeying my commands. It's what turns me on. I can learn to read your body signals and know when you need more. When you trust me with your submission, you're handing me my power. Do you understand?"

"In theory."

"We'll find out this weekend at Eden. I hope you're ready to play, Sweet. I know I am."

CHAPTER 12

I HADN'T RECEIVED any phone calls or letters from Evan recently, and that made me nervous. If he was quiet, it meant he was most likely plotting. I'd taken every precaution.

Tonight, though, I had no intention of thinking about, or worrying over, him. When I pulled into Penny's driveway I noticed the surveillance car parked across the street. Now, I stood with my fingers drumming against my leg in an impatient gesture while I waited for her to answer.

Suddenly, the door swung open and I almost swallowed my tongue. Covering part of her face was a small black and purple masquerade mask. She wore a matching deep purple, almost black, knee-length halter dress that accentuated her hourglass figure. What made it stunning was the keyhole cut out, big enough to see the swell of her breasts and dipped low enough to see the shadow between them, but small enough to still keep everything covered. It offered a tease of what to expect beneath the dress and made me want to tear the fucking thing off with my teeth.

I had to clear my throat before greeting her. "You look absolutely stunning, Sweet. I'm curious though. Which deadly sin are you representing? Because if I had to take a guess, it would be lust."

She ducked her head, and the pink that was quickly becoming my favorite color spread across her cheekbones. "Thank you, Marcus. I was kind of going for envy, because I want women to be envious of the fact that I'm with you tonight."

Her shy reply gave me an instant hard on. "Well, if that's the case, I'm representing pride, because I'm a Dom proud of his sub."

Penny looked up at me from beneath lowered lashes. "Am I?"

"Are you what?"

"Your sub?"

There was almost a hint of hope in her question. With a single finger under her chin, I raised her head up so she was looking directly at me.

"As long as you're exploring this lifestyle, then, yes, I'm your Dom."

I offered her my arm. "Shall we?"

She didn't hesitate to slide her hand through. "Yes, Sir."

Arm in arm, I escorted her to my car. When I took off down the street, I noticed the surveillance vehicle pull away from the curb and stay a close distance behind us. Soon, we arrived at the familiar warehouse district. I parked the car and we walked across the street to Eden's front door. As usual, Philip granted us entrance. Penny avidly avoided looking at the desk in the foyer, which had me chuckling. I threaded our fingers and we made our way down the hall to the public playroom.

Soft music played throughout the area, and the crowd was on the light side since it was still relatively early. We wandered around the room admiring the various costumes when a feminine voice called out Penny's name.

We turned to see Bridget making her way toward us wearing an emerald green corset, barely there underwear, and a complementary green and black masquerade mask. Unlike my date's though, hers had several large attached feathers. When Bridget reached us, she ignored me entirely and pulled Penny in for a hug. She pulled back and her eyes scanned up and down, admiring the other woman.

"Damn, you look smoking hot. I adore this dress on you. Turn," —she gestured with a finger — "and let me see the whole thing."

To my surprise, Penny glanced up at me like she was seeking permission.

She released her hold on my hand and twirled in a circle giving Bridget, who whistled in appreciation, the view she requested.

"So, I meet with your approval then?" I noticed Penny's hands surreptitiously smoothing the fabric of her dress in a nervous gesture.

Bridget's hands went to her hips. "You certainly don't need my approval, but if you did, hell yeah you have it. Jesus, I'm envious of your curves. Which is appropriate since I came as envy tonight."

Mimicking Penny, she also gave a little spin. I spotted

Connor over the women's heads and he gestured for me to join him.

"Ladies, I'm going to leave you to chat for a bit. Bridget, I expect you to behave like a proper sub and don't teach my sub here any of your bad habits. One brat in my life is enough. If you can't do that, I'm sure I can find a strong enough Dom somewhere who can teach you how to act."

Ignoring her overdramatic eye roll, I moved into Penny's personal space, causing her to look up at me. I cupped her cheek. "You're welcome to mingle with any of the other submissives Bridget introduces you to, however, you are not to engage with any Doms should one approach you other than to tell them you're here with me. Understood?"

She placed her palm over mine. "Yes, Sir."

"And since she will do everything to ignore the warning I just gave, I'll remind you since you're the one sub I have power over. Brats get punished while good subs get rewarded. Think about which one you'd like most."

Leaving her to ponder her decision, I left the two women alone and headed toward the bar where Connor waited, his eyes glued to Bridget. I took the opportunity to study my friend. He was built like a linebacker, massive and muscled. He wasn't handsome in the typical sense; his face was too craggy, but he had a certain ruggedness that had the subs at Eden vying for his attention. He didn't play publicly. He always took the few subs I'd seen him with into one of the private rooms.

I slid onto the bar stool next to him and sent him a pointed stare. His attention shifted to me, and I could tell he was now all business.

"I might have a lead on Evan."

I straightened at the news.

"Josie discovered a communication from one of our office computers to him. She's looking into who accessed that particular PC. It might take her a few days. I have less than thirty employees who have unlimited access to the majority of the technology we use, minus a few exceptions. But, I do have a few contractors who come into the office. This was a general office computer that anyone one could have logged into. After this, I plan on updating all the login protocols and decreasing access."

"Keep me posted, will you?"

"Of course."

I held up my hand to signal the bartender. I ordered a Corona and a gin and tonic. Once he'd brought, I picked them both up and glanced at Connor.

"Word of advice?"

He stared back warily.

"She's more than most Doms can handle, but she's fiercely loyal and will do anything for those she loves. I'm not sure what's holding you back, but if there's something there, you need to go for it, man."

I didn't wait for a response. Instead, I turned and headed back over to where Bridget and Penny stood, anxious to see where tonight would lead us.

CHAPTER 13

"So, how are things between you and Marcus now that the whole Evan thing is out in the open?"

I wasn't sure how to respond. "It's been a little awkward. I mean, I'm still really pissed that I'm basically being stalked by some lunatic with a vendetta against him, but I also understand he tried to keep me out of it. It just happened too late."

I could tell Bridget sympathized with me. "I get it. I mean, I didn't even know Grace, but the minute I found out that some piece of shit ex beat her up, I knew I had to help her. There's nothing I hate more than some pissant little fucker thinking he can get away with hitting a woman. For the brief time she stayed with me, I got to know her a little bit. She's a nice woman who doesn't deserve this psychopath chasing after her. And you don't deserve to be caught in the middle either. I'm sorry that you are."

I reached out to hug her. "I appreciate that. I will admit that ever since Evan made contact Marcus has shifted into protective Dom mode. Never would I have expected that to be a total turn-on."

It was freeing to be able to discuss the topic so openly with another woman who would understand exactly how I was feeling. Bridget was an experienced submissive, and I was glad I had someone to talk to about these things.

"Lord, you have no idea. There's nothing sexier than when your Dom gets all growly and fierce. It's like instant puddle."

I laughed at her description, because it was spot on. "What about you? How come you don't have a Dom?"

Her eyes flashed with pain, before she quickly wiped it away. "I can't be tied down to just one Dominant. There are too many choices out there to settle. I like that each one I scene with brings something different to the table. Besides, I don't think there's any Dom out there who could handle me."

Her response seemed too flippant, too rehearsed to be true, but something in her tone made me not want to push further. It just made me wonder what the truth was.

"I admire your independence. Your confidence. I wish I had half of it."

Bridget drew back in outrage. "Oh my god, you're crazy. You should be bathing in confidence. You're absolutely gorgeous with that natural auburn hair. And those curves? I'd kill for your body. I have tits, but my hips are non-existent. You have that perfect hourglass shape. If I even thought for a second you might be bi-sexual or hetero-flexible, I'd be making a pass at you for sure."

My mouth dropped open and I didn't know what to say.

She burst out laughing. "You should see your face. Girl,

you are absolutely freaked out right now. I just wanted to show you how amazing you are. Marcus better realize how lucky he is."

"I feel like I'm the lucky one. These last few weeks have been nothing like anything I'd have ever thought I'd be a part of. And I don't mean the Evan shit. I mean this--" I threw my arm out to encompass the whole club. "Even as nervous and slightly uncomfortable I've felt at times, I feel like this is where I was always meant to be."

She reached out for my hand. "Because it is. When you know, you know. I've never in my life met another more accepting group of people. No one judges you. You can just be yourself with no fear. It's the most amazing feeling ever."

We stood there for a moment, enjoying the friendship we'd discovered. Bridget squeezed my hand before releasing it.

"Now, tell me one thing you're dying to try with Marcus."

And just like that I was flustered again. "Um... I'm not sure."

Immediately, her hands went to her hips and she stared me down with a look. One that said she wasn't hearing my bullshit.

"Fine," I harumphed. "I want to see what the flogger feels like."

Bridget clapped her hands in excitement. "Yummy. The flogger is one of my favorite things. The thwap of the falls hitting my skin and then the warm sensation across my skin that follows. Mmmm, it's the most delicious feeling in the world."

"Really? It doesn't hurt?" I questioned.

"It's a delicious hurt. Promise. It stings a little if whoever's wielding it hits the right spot. It's more thuddy though. I have a feeling you're going to become a flogger slut."

I coughed and almost choked at that. "A flogger slut?"

She winked. "Most definitely. You're gonna get one taste and fall in love. You'll never get enough of it."

My mind tried to wrap itself around the image she created, but I couldn't do it. It was obviously one of those things I would need to experience first.

"She'll never get enough of what?"

I spun around with a squeal of surprise. Bridget merely chuckled.

"I was just telling your beautiful sub here about the wondrous implement known as the flogger."

Marcus perked up in interest. "Oh, really? That's funny, she and I had an almost similar conversation recently."

Bridget huffed. "You were holding out on me."

I couldn't help the flush that crawled up my neck. "I wasn't holding out. You asked me a question, and I answered."

"Ladies, I hate to interrupt, but I'd like to have my sub all to myself if you don't mind."

If I hadn't sensed the sarcasm in Marcus' tone, the look he sent Bridget would have clued me in. He really wasn't asking. She obviously heard it as well, and for once, she acquiesced without putting up much of a fuss.

"Of course."

She gave me a hug and after she kissed me on the cheek, she whispered in my ear. "You're going to have the best orgasms of your life tonight. Enjoy the flogger, babe."

I inhaled sharply and coughed even as she sashayed

across the room with an exaggerated swing to her hips. She turned her head, winked, and continued strutting across the club like she owned it.

"What did she say to you?" Marcus' breath tickled my ear.

I hadn't realized he'd move so close, but I noticed now, his chest brushing against my arm.

"Noth...nothing," I stuttered.

He stepped back and crossed his arms. "Oh, really? Are you sure that's the answer you want to go with? Might I remind you what happens to subs who are good?"

My voice was hesitant. "They get rewarded?"

"Exactly. Now, would you like to change your response?" He raised an eyebrow.

I paused and reflected a moment. I discovered I really wanted that reward, even if I didn't yet know what that entailed. I cleared my throat.

"She told me to enjoy the flogger and the multiple orgasms you were going to give me."

Now it seemed to be Marcus' turn to choke on laughter. "It seems like Bridget just issued a challenge on your behalf. I guess I'll have to make sure I deliver."

He held out his hand. "Are you ready for your reward now?"

I didn't hesitate. I answered by placing my hand in his. I was ready for this man to lead me into ruin.

CHAPTER 14

I LED Penny toward the back of the public area where Leo, a dungeon monitor, stood guard at the entrance of a wide hallway. Down both walls were doors evenly spaced apart. When we stopped in front of the room I'd requested, I opened the door and ushered her in. Decadent described it perfectly.

Silk fabric wallpaper covered the walls and the king-size canopy bed dominated the center of the room with its plush headboard and burgundy satin fabric covering. Silks and satin fabrics including yards of it hanging from the thick canopy and its matching posters decorated the entire room. It was made to have the look of wealth without being tacky.

"Let's get you more comfortable."

I guided Penny to the foot of the bed where I removed her half mask and gently tossed it on the wooden chest near where we stood. Then I bent down on one knee. She balanced her hand on my shoulder when I picked up her left foot and removed her shoe. She wobbled a little, when

I slid my hand up her calf and thigh, the fabric of her dress rising with the movement. I could feel the heat of her body, but I stopped mid-thigh lightly caressing the back of her leg with a single fingertip. She shivered at my touch. I looked up and our eyes met as she stared down at me. Her lips were parted and her chest rapidly rose and fell. With a final caress to that leg, I switched to the other one, only this time, my fingers moved downward until I reached her second shoe. Again, she steadied herself when she raised her other leg. Now barefoot, she wiggled her bare toes like she was relieved to finally be out of the heels. I stood and looked down at her.

"We've discussed your limits, but now it's time for a safeword. Do you have one?"

Penny's eyes widened slightly like she was panicked. I tried to reassure her. "If you can't think of one, it's not a big deal. The standard club safeword is 'red'. If you think you can remember that, it's a perfectly acceptable one to use. The minute you say it, whatever we're doing stops. No matter what."

Instantly Penny's expression changed to one of relief. "I'll use red then."

I cupped her cheek. "This is all new to you, and I understand that. Don't be afraid to use it or think you'll disappoint me. Got it?"

She responded solemnly. "Yes, Sir."

"Perfect. If there's something I'm doing that you're unsure of and you need to slow down, you can use yellow. I'll ease off and we can talk about what's happening and decide where to go from there. Green means all's good. Understood?"

"Yes, Sir," she repeated.

"I told you what hearing those words from your lips do to me. You've been such a good sub, it's time you were rewarded."

Unable to wait any longer, I dipped my head and crushed my lips against hers. My tongue edged its way into her mouth, and I deepened the kiss, drinking her all in. Her tongue tangled with mine, and I clutched her hip pulling her against me. Penny whimpered and pressed herself even closer, almost undulated against my erection. My grip instinctively tightened, and I briefly wondered if I'd leave bruises on her skin. The kiss went on and on while we learned each other's taste. I pulled away and rested my forehead against hers, our breathing sounding harsh in the quiet.

"Turn around," I directed.

She heeded my command and presented me with her back. I reached up to sweep the hair off her neck and unzipped her dress. Peppering kisses down her spine, I stopped where the zipper ended just above the curve of her ass. Penny shivered in response. Using just my fingertips, I pushed the the dress off her shoulders, my fingers trailing down her arms before reaching to wear the fabric bunched at her hips. With nothing but a gentle tug, the dress slid over them and then fell to a puddle on the floor at her feet. I stepped around to face her.

Before me stood a goddess, cloaked now in only a bra and the tiniest scrap of cloth covering her mound. Her gaze met mine for an instant and then she lowered her eyes to the floor, her chest and face flushed red. Her fists were clenched tight against her hips, and I knew she was fighting the urge to cover herself.

"You're a vision. I could stand here and stare at you all

night long. Absolutely gorgeous, and I can't wait to fuck you."

With just those words, Penny's entire body relaxed and she looked up at me with a shy smile. "I can't wait either. Sir."

On that last, delayed syllable, there was a sultry tone in her voice that hardened my cock even further. She was playing the innocent seductress role so well. Without wasting another moment, I circled back behind her and unclasped her bra, letting it fall to the floor. I held out my hand and she stepped out of the pooled dress. Then, I directed her to the bed.

"Grab that poster," I pointed at the bed's wooden pillar nearest her. She hesitated only briefly before planting her feet slightly apart and bending the tiniest bit forward. She wrapped her hands around the thick square poster of the canopy bed and arched her back. Her juicy ass was on full display. I was surprised at how she had positioned herself almost intuitively based on my brief instruction.

I stepped over to the wardrobe full of various implements and opened the door, searching for a specific one. I removed the black flogger from the hook and admired the craftsmanship of its design. Lightly, I slapped the falls across the palm of my hand and ran my fingers through them, breathing in the leather scent, feeling the dynamic shift. The Dom within me was ready to come out and play. I glanced over at Penny who remained in the same position I'd left her. In my head I pictured her reddened back and ass and my hand tingled with the need to wield the implement.

"What's your safe word?" I strode back to her and

traced my finger down her spine. Gooseflesh pebbled on her arms.

"Red, Sir," she breathed out.

I held up the flogger for her to see it up close. "I'm sure you recognize this from your first visit here."

She took it in and nodded almost eagerly. "Yes, Sir, I remember it well."

"Wonderful. Now, don't let go," I warned as I brushed the falls of the flogger across her back on either side of her spine to give her a feel for the sensation. Up and down I stroked and then I stepped away. Then my wrist moved in a familiar figure eight pattern and soon I had the perfect rhythm going. I moved forward and lightly, I continued my wrist movement. The *whoosh* of leather through the air followed by the light *thwap* of the falls hitting flesh gave me a rush like no other.

I held back at first, like a loving caress. With each pass, the force of my strokes grew stronger. My cock hardened as the pink colors brightened to red with each of the flogger's falls. When I'd reached the perfect shade, I stopped and checked on Penny. Her eyes were slightly glassy.

"What color are we, sub?"

"Green, Sir." She exhaled her words.

I leaned in to whisper in her ear, and I could feel the heat radiating off her back. "If I were to slide my fingers through your pussy lips, would I find you wet?"

All she could do was nod her assent.

"Let's see if you're right."

I pressed my chest against Penny's back and reached around her waist, my fingers slipping inside the elastic waistband of the small scrap of fabric she still wore. True to her word, her cunt was dripping. One digit found her clit, and I began a slow circular movement over the bundle of nerves. She whimpered, but remained holding onto the poster. I gathered more moisture from her slit and continued my assault on the hooded nub. She pushed against me and gasped.

"I want to fuck you so hard you'll forget every man who has ever fucked you before." My voice was raspy with need.

"I want that too, Sir," Penny breathed out. "I want you to fuck me. I don't know what you've done to me. You're all I think about. It's like you've cast a spell on me. I want to submit to you. Please."

That was the only consent I needed. I plunged two fingers into her juicy cunt and worked them in and out. The tension built in her until, with a single brush of my thumb over her clit, her back arched and her whole body shuddered. Mewling sounds escaped her throat as the orgasm rushed through her. Her knees gave out and I pulled her against my chest to keep her upright.

"You're beautiful." I whispered into her ear. "Did you like your reward?"

She sighed drowsily even as she nodded. "Most definitely. Thank you, Sir."

"That's a good thing, because it's not over yet. I want you on your back on the bed."

Gathering her strength, Penny straightened, and I playfully swatted her ass. She squeaked and rubbed it while she followed my instructions. Tossing the flogger aside, I hurriedly disrobed and grabbed a condom out of the night stand. I watched her position herself and finally her gaze landed on me. She inhaled sharply at the sight of me standing there naked.

Penny's eyes traveled the length of my body and then zeroed in on my erect cock. I sensed the shift in her breathing. Slowly, I walked with purpose toward where she lay. When I climbed onto the bed and straddled her legs, her eyes locked onto mine. With a light touch, I slid my hands under her knees and lifted, coaxing them to bend toward her chest. I traced a path down her hips before hooking my thumbs under the satin fabric covering her sex. Gently, I tugged.

"Lift up," I commanded when they snagged.

Penny raised her butt and I pulled them over hips, continuing to lowering them until they were completely removed. Then I tossed them onto the floor. Her breathing grew even more shallow when I separated her knees. Finally I broke our visual connection so my eyes could take in the beauty on full display.

"I wish you could see yourself right now splayed out for me. Your pussy is so wet and pink. I want to eat it and lick up all your juice." My mouth watered just thinking about it.

I glanced up and her eyes were the color of a midnight sky. She was almost panting now.

"I'll save that for later, because right now, I need to be inside you."

"Please."

That single word was my undoing.

Snatching up the condom, I tore open the wrapper and slid it down my throbbing length. Then I moved over her and at the same time I slammed my mouth down on hers, I thrust my cock inside her cunt embedding it all the way to the hilt.

Penny gasped at the sensation while I groaned from

deep in my chest at the feel of her tightness surrounding me. God the sensation was amazing. When I gained control, I started to move. In and out I thrust, gaining momentum with each push and pull. All the while, I continued my assault on her lips. My tongue mimicked the movement of my cock, and I moaned every time she clenched down on me. I didn't think I was going to last long.

I slid my hand between us and played with her clit as I continued to thrust in and out. Penny pushed up against me with each forward thrust of my cock.

"You have no idea how much you turn me on," I mumbled against her lips. " I could fuck you forever. This soft, sweet pussy of yours was made to be filled by me."

The muscles in her body tightened, and I knew her orgasm was seconds away. Increasing the pressure on her clit, I quickened my thrusts as my balls drew up. I was about to explode, but she needed to come first. My prayers were answered when her pussy contracted against my dick, and the orgasm rushed through her. She threw her head back and screamed my name with the force of it. At the same time, my cock erupted as her pussy continued to milk me.

When the final tremor ceased, I half collapsed on top of her, keeping my full weight off her with my elbows. Our breathing was harsh in the empty room. I brushed her hair back off her sweat-dampened forehead and brush a kiss across her lips before pulling out and rolling onto my side. I lay there for a moment, trying to capture my breath. I turned my head to glance over at her. The look of satisfied pleasure on Penny's face was intoxicating.

I rose from the bed and discarded the condom before

crawling back in beside her. I pulled her body close to mine, whispering words of approval and kissing her on the forehead. She wrapped herself around me and closed her eyes as I continued speaking softly to her. Within moments, a small sigh left her lips and her entire body relaxed.

I lay with my hand behind my head as I stared at the ceiling, reliving the most intense orgasm I could remember having. There were so many feelings she brought out in me. Her submissive nature called out to my Dominant side on so many levels. Not the least of which was the need to protect her from Evan. But there was more. Feelings that made me nervous. I wanted to guide her, mentor her, until she finally recognized what a powerful submissive she truly was. I wanted to watch her bloom and grow like a well-tended flower.

I felt her stir beside me. I turned my head when she shifted a little. She laid there with a dreamy smile on her face, her arm across my chest as she snuggled closer, and I was fucked. Somehow she'd snuck past my defenses and made me care. I hated to wake her, but it was getting late, and I needed to get her home. I reached out and caressed her arms.

"Wake up, little sub."

She twitched and slowly came awake, struggling to open her eyes. Once she finally gained control and focused, her gaze locked on mine and a sleepy smile spread across her face. *Damn, she was gorgeous.*

"Sorry I fell asleep."

"I'm going to assume that means I just wore you out so much with your reward."

She giggled. "Oh, you most definitely did. That was the

best reward ever."

I leaned down to kiss her. "Good. Are you ready to get up yet?"

"If I have to." She stretched like a cat, her breasts thrust upward and tempting me all over again, but it was getting late.

We rose and after we were both dressed, we made our way back out to the public area, letting Leo, who remained on duty, know that the room and implement needed to be sanitized. Briefly, Penny searched for Bridget, but she was nowhere in sight.

Arm in arm, we headed to my car. "How about dinner at my house tomorrow night?"

She glanced up at me. "I'd like that."

"Wonderful. I'll text you my address in the morning."

I drove her home, holding her hand the entire way. While I escorted her to the door, her security guard parked his car in front of the house.

"Thank you for a wonderful evening, Marcus."

"You're most welcome."

She stood there looking irresistible in the moonlight that I couldn't help but have another taste. I dipped my head for a final goodnight kiss. Reluctantly, I broke it off.

"Good night. See you tomorrow."

She gave a small wave as she disappeared inside.

I walked to my car and just before I reached it, headlights of another vehicle drew closer. The black SUV slowed and as it passed the driver's side window lowered, revealing Evan's leering expression. He hiked his chin up in a mocking gesture, speeding off before I could even dive behind the wheel to give chase.

Son of a bitch.

CHAPTER 15

IRRITATED, I stood in front of Marcus' front door. I'd woken up this morning for work to not only a text message from him with his address, but also to the news that my security detail had doubled. When I asked why, I was only told by Connor that extra precautions were being taken. Needless to say, I was pretty pissed off. This was my life and I wanted answers. Ones I planned on getting tonight. Knocking loudly, I waited for Marcus to answer at the same time I kept glancing over my shoulder, my eyes scanning the street for some threat.

Only moments later, he opened the front door. Without waiting for an invitation, I pushed past him.

"Come in," he said, drily.

Still fuming, I paced, criss-crossing back and forth across his living room. When I finally felt like my anger was under control, I turned to find him standing there, arms crossed, with an eyebrow raised and a look I was afraid to interpret on his face. I swallowed nervously, my anger mellowing a little as another more prominent emotion pushed back.

"Are you finished with your tantrum and ready to explain what has you all fired up?"

The word 'tantrum', like I was a child throwing a fit, had the steam rising inside me again.

Mimicking Marcus' pose I faced off against him. "No one is telling me why I now have more security. I'm pretty sure I have the right to know."

He stalked forward slowly, and instinctively, I took a step back, but then forced myself to stop. My head tipped back when he finally came abreast of me.

"Have you asked me?" Marcus stared down his nose at me, disappointment in his eyes.

I swallowed again. "Um, no."

When he didn't respond, I realized he was waiting for me to ask.

"Can you tell me why I have extra security?"

He cleared his throat expectantly.

"Please?" I tacked on when it hit me what he was waiting on.

"Just as I was about to leave your house last night, Evan drove by. He wanted me to know he was in the neighborhood. I thought it prudent that, considering he now knew where you lived, additional precautions be taken to ensure your safety. If you'd asked me politely when you arrived instead of storming in here so rudely, I would have explained it to you sooner."

I flushed guiltily. "I'm sorry."

"Oh, you will be." Promise tinged his words at the same time he gripped my arm and pulled me over to the couch. He sat down and before I guessed his intent, he tugged my arm and I landed across his lap, my ass in the air.

"What are you doing?" I struggled to gain my balance, but a hand across my upper back and stinging slap to my ass had me reaching back to soothe it.

"I'm punishing you," came the reply from above my head.

"You can't do that," I screeched, still straining to stand from my face down position.

Another stinging swat to my ass froze me in place.

"I'm afraid that's where you're wrong, Penny. I'm your Dom, and it's my job to punish you as I see fit. Your insolence is certainly deserving of one. I understand your anger, but to so rudely enter my home was uncalled for. I don't tolerate brats. Had you simply asked me your question like an adult, I would have obliged you."

"You're right. I'm sorry," I repeated.

He gently placed his hand on my ass. "I appreciate the apology, but it doesn't negate the fact that you were a brat and have to face the consequences of your actions. Now, are you ready to receive your punishment?"

I hesitated, but finally nodded. "Yes, Sir."

I tensed in preparation, but nothing happened. Just when I relaxed, the first blow landed on my right ass cheek. I flinched at the pain and reached back to rub it.

"If you move your hand another inch, I'll be adding onto your infraction. And I'm pretty sure you don't want that."

My arm froze at the growled words. Slowly, reluctantly, I lowered it. Then came the second strike.

"That was two. Now, you count."

The next two were in rapid succession, and he alternated where they landed.

"Damn, those hurt." I squirmed .

A sharp pinch in the same spot he'd last struck caused me to cry out. "I said to count. Do I need to add more to your punishment?"

I rapidly shook my head. "No, Sir. The pain distracted me. I won't forget again. Three and four."

The pain eased when Marcus lovingly caressed my ass through my dress. Before I could take my next breath, cool air blew across my backside when he flipped the fabric up to expose me to his view. I almost reached back, but at the last minute recalled his warning.

Another strike landed, this one harder than the four prior. I barely remembered to count.

"Five," I gasped out.

He rubbed and massaged my bare ass and the pain immediately went away. Pleasure replaced it. Enough pleasure that I began to squirm for a different reason. Marcus' hand glided down the slope of my ass and rested in the crease of my thigh, dangerously close to my core.

"I think you might be enjoying your punishment more than you're admitting, little sub."

His hand shifted and I gasped when one of his fingers brushed up against my wet heat.

"I've been extremely easy on you until now. I want you to associate pleasure with some pain. This is punishment, so you can't enjoy it too much. You have to understand the consequences of your actions. Get ready, because for these last ten, I'm not going to be easy on you. You won't enjoy this."

With that pronouncement, he struck. In rapid succession, his hand landed hard on alternating cheeks, some in the same spot as the last. Each blow landed harder than the one before it, and I struggled and fought against each one, narrowly remembering to count each strike. By the tenth, I was sobbing openly. Marcus abruptly stopped, perhaps to prolong my agony a little longer. It made me think maybe he had a touch of sadist in him. That thought, more than anything, made me nervous.

"I know this is your first punishment, and I'm so proud of how well you've taken it, Penny. You'll do the same with these last five," he said with confidence.

Thankfully, he put me out of my misery and administered them so quickly, I could barely keep up with the count.

"Fifteen," I screamed as the last blow struck, tears blinding me.

Marcus soothed my ass, earning a flinch. Then, he gently helped me to my feet before pulling me down so I sat on his lap. I gasped and tried to buck myself off from the pain, but he only wrapped his arms around me in comfort as I bawled. I lost track of time as we sat together, but eventually my sobs quieted. He stroked the hair off my face and wiped away a lone tear that remained.

"I'm sorry I had to punish you, Sweetness. It's never easy the first time, or any other time, in fact. Just part of the learning process. You accepted it beautifully though."

With one last sniff, I swiped my palm over my eyes, taking the last bit of moisture, and peered up at him. "I hated that. Well, the first couple were okay. The rest were agony I never want to experience again."

Marcus laughed softly at my expression. "I hate to break it to you, but there is no doubt that, at some point in time, you're going to be punished again for some infraction or another."

"God, I hope not. That sucked," I whined.

He chuckled at my pout. "Only time will tell. Now that we've gotten that out of the way, are you ready for a nice dinner?"

"That's it?"

"What do you mean?" Marcus asked.

"You were pretty peeved at me and now you're… over it?" I didn't understand.

He stroked my cheek with his thumb. "That's how a punishment works. I was irritated, but not raging. I would never strike you in true anger. Your behavior has received correction, and now we move on to more pleasant things. That's how it works."

"I see." I didn't. Not really, but I wasn't going to argue.

It was obvious Marcus didn't believe me. "You'll figure it out eventually. So… dinner?"

My stomach rumbling answered his question, and I laughed. "I guess so."

"Good. I made lasagna. I hope you like it."

He nudged me and I rose off his lap, with him following behind. Linking our fingers, we walked into the kitchen where lit candles graced the table and a beautiful vase of roses served as the centerpiece. He let loose of my hand and pulled out my chair for me.

"Let me check on the food and grab a bottle of wine. Sit and relax."

I sat and watched him work. The man seemed to know what he was doing. It was fascinating, and oddly arousing, seeing Marcus at ease in here. He pulled the food out of the oven and set it on a hotplate. Then, he uncorked the wine and poured two glasses before setting one in front of me and the other at his place setting. Next came our plates. He picked up his wine glass and I followed suit.

"To an amazing woman. May you receive all the things in life you want and deserve."

My chest ached at his toast. It was so earnest and sincere. "Thank you, Marcus."

His smile was big and bright. "You're more than welcome, Sweet."

My heart skipped a beat, and in that moment I fell. Hard.

CHAPTER 16

PENNY and I enjoyed a lovely dinner, but my mind occasionally drifted to Evan. Connor had called this morning to let me know Josie thought she'd discovered who had communicated with him through email. They were questioning one of the company's newest employees. Once they confirmed it was her, hopefully it would lead to finding where Evan was hiding out. In the meantime, it continued to be a waiting game. One I was getting sorely tired of. I understood Penny's frustrations. I wasn't going to dwell on shit right now. Instead, I was going to focus on this woman in front of me.

I knew I was falling for her. How could I not? Her innate submissive side spoke to my Dominant one. She gave off this energy that was warm and inviting. She seemed confident, but I sensed her struggle sometimes.

"You came to that first munch for a reason. You said it was to explore this lifestyle. Do you mean to tell me that none of your other partners were willing?"

She set her wine glass down. "I haven't been with anyone in five years."

My eyes widened in shock, but I quickly recovered. I didn't want her to think there was anything wrong with that. I was just surprised.

"And the last man I was with was pretty much a piece of shit," she continued.

I coughed to cover my laughter. "I see."

Penny briefly glanced at me before turning her eyes downcast to her plate. She played with the food on her plate, pushing it around, looking at it, but not really seeing it. Suddenly, I didn't think it was so funny anymore. I reached out to cover her hand with mine and she looked up at me before setting down her fork.

"Would you like to tell me about it?" I asked.

She shrugged. "Same sad story, I guess. Throughout our entire relationship, my ex told me I was fat. That I wasn't smart enough or good enough. It was so subtle though, I didn't even realize it was happening until one night when we were out with some friends. I'd come back from the bathroom to hear him talking to one of his buddies. They were laughing and joking about how he had to turn the lights off when we had sex, because he couldn't stand to look at me. He even commented on the number of side chicks he had. At that point, I realized what I'd allowed him to do to me and my self-esteem. I felt so stupid for being oblivious to how I'd allowed him to treat me. That moment defined me and made me realize that I deserved better. Without a word, I walked out of the bar and never saw him again."

Rage coursed through me at this unknown man and the fact that he didn't see what I saw. A pure, innocent woman who encompassed everything I didn't even know I'd wanted.

"You're right. He is a piece of shit."

She smiled sadly, like she didn't believe me.

"I think it's time for dessert."

She wiped her mouth with her napkin and shook her head. "Oh, no, thank you. I couldn't eat another bite. Dinner was delicious. Thank you."

"I wasn't talking about you."

Slowly, Penny lowered the cloth to her lap with a crinkle between her brows. I stood and towered over her.

"Up." I gestured with my finger.

After a moment's hesitation, she rose from her chair. I pulled her over to the kitchen island. She yelped in surprise when I placed my hands around her waist and boosted her up so she sat on the counter top.

"Marcus!" She squeaked when I pulled her blouse over head.

I swatted her thigh when she reached up to cover herself. "Hands at your sides."

She huffed, but complied.

"Now, don't move."

Not waiting to see if she obeyed, I turned and opened the fridge. I rifled through the items in the door until I found what I was looking for. Grabbing two things, I returned to stand in front of her. Penny's eyes widened when she spotted what I'd set on the counter next to her.

"Wha... what is that for?" she stuttered.

One side of my mouth tipped up. "I think you know exactly what it's for."

She shook her head. "Oh, no. Marcus, no."

"Oh, yes. Take off your bra." My voice broke no argument.

I sensed her indecision, but I remained patient. Barely. She let out a long sigh and then twisted her arms behind her before sliding the straps down her shoulders. I took it out of her hands and threw it on the table behind me.

Her eyes followed me as I shook the canister before popping off the lid. I held the nozzle up to her breast and pressed, causing whipped cream to spray out across her skin. I leaned down and lapped it up with my tongue. Her body was tense. I repeated the action to her other breast. Back and forth I decorated her skin with whipped cream, taking my time and savoring the cold, sweet flavor.

I separated Penny's knees, stepped between them, set the canister on the counter and threaded my fingers through her hair before crushing my mouth against hers. I tasted the wine on her tongue along with the whipped cream that still lingered on mine. Our tongues dueled, and I moved my hand to cradle her face between my palms while she reached up and ran her fingers through my hair.

My mouth captured the gasps and noises coming from her throat. Inch by inch, I trailed kisses mixed with love bites down her neck, making sure I hit the sensitive spot behind her ears. I rubbed my scruff across her skin, sending a shiver through her, and she moaned in pleasure. My hands traced a path down her arms until my palms flattened against the counter on the outside of her hips, and I caged her between my arms.

I moved further south until I reached her breasts again. Taking my time, I tugged first one nipple, then the other between my teeth. Needing more, I unbuttoned her jeans and pulled.

"Shift."

She raised one hip then the other while I tugged her jeans and underwear down and tossed them off to the side.

"Lean back on your elbows." My voice was guttural with arousal at the sight of Penny's nakedness.

When she immediately followed my command, I praised her, spread her legs even further, and grabbed the other item I'd pulled from the fridge.

She yelped when I squeezed the cold chocolate syrup right on her sex.

Our eyes met and remained connected as I squatted down, looped my hands under her thighs, and flicked my tongue up her pussy lips, taking the chocolate with me that had dripped down her slit. I repeated my action until I'd licked her clean, savoring every last drop.

I tasted a mixture of chocolate and Penny's sweet pussy juice on my tongue. I wanted more. Once again I poured syrup over her. She threw her head back when I feasted again. This time, I sucked her clit, flicking it with my tongue and nibbling it with my teeth. She was panting now, and I knew her release was hovering on the edge. Wanting to send her toppling over it, I slipped a single digit inside her and began to piston it back and forth. When I added another finger and curled them, she cried out my name. I repeated my action at the same time I bit down hard on her clit. Her leg muscles tightened and her toes curled as she screamed out her climax.

Penny's elbows gave out and she collapsed onto her back, her chest rapidly rising and falling. I licked all the flavors off my lips and made a satisfied, smacking noise with them. She raised her head to look at me with glazed eyes full of pleasure. I held out a hand to her and helped her sit back up. She hopped down off the counter, her legs trembling.

"That was the best dessert I think I've ever had," I said with a self-satisfied grin.

She blushed and dipped her head. "I'm glad you enjoyed it."

I tipped her chin up and kissed her, letting her taste the mixture of flavors I'd just savored.

"Why don't you go upstairs and take a shower. You can use the master bath. Last door on the left. I'm going to clean up down here, and then I'll be up shortly."

Penny nodded. "Yes, Sir."

She snatched up all her discarded clothes and walked out of the kitchen toward the stairs. I put away the whipped cream and chocolate with a smile and then washed all the dishes. After drying my hands, I grabbed one thing and headed up to see how my lovely sub was doing. I had so much more planned for the night.

CHAPTER 17

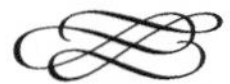

AFTER A HOT SHOWER, I found myself alone in Marcus' room. Wrapped in a towel, I surveyed my surroundings. The room was extremely masculine, from the recessed ceiling made of medium shaded wood paneling to the basic, eggshell colored walls. One of the walls housed double doors, which I briefly peeked into, that opened to a full walk-in closet. The opposite wall drew my complete attention. Covering almost its entirety was a giant gilt-framed mirror. The only space on the wall that the mirror didn't cover was the doorway leading out into the rest of the house. A doorway Marcus just stepped through.

We stared at each other for several heartbeats, arousal thick between us. I would never get tired of looking at this man.

"Thank you for letting me use your shower. As much fun as the food play was earlier, it's much better being clean."

"You are welcome to anything in my home, Penny. As

long as I'm your Dom and you belong to me, you have full reign of the house."

"Thank you, Marcus." My heart leapt at the thought of belonging to him. I forced it to slow down though. He'd been protective, like I suspected a good Dom was supposed to be, and yes, I was falling for him, but that didn't mean he felt the same way. I wasn't even sure I wanted him to. All of this was still new, and I was enjoying exploring and trying out new things. So, for now, I just planned on taking each day as it came.

Right now, seeing him standing there, I wanted to kiss him. I smiled what I hoped was seductively, and propelled myself forward until I was toe to toe with him. It wasn't until I reached him that I noticed he had an insulated ice bucket in his hand, similar to one used to chill a bottle of wine.

"What's that for?"

"You'll see," he said as he reached out.

Marcus yanked on the towel wrapped around me, and I let it fall to the floor. He took my hand and directed me to the king-sized bed.

"I want you to lie down on your back," Marcus directed me.

Following his request, I positioned myself and wondered where this night would lead to next. I watched as he reached into the bedside table and pulled out several cords made of black silk.

"Give me your hands."

Trustingly, I stretched my arms forward. After tying a loose knot around my wrists with the cords, he then secured each of my arms to the top two posters with the remaining length of cord.

"You remember your safe word?"

I nodded. "Yes, Sir. It's red."

"Good girl."

He pulled my legs up one by one so they were bent toward my chest. Using extra long lengths of the cords, my legs were also bound to the posts with the cord behind my knees to keep me open and exposed to his heated gaze. I was vulnerable and completely at his mercy. I knew my safe word, but I wanted everything he was offering.

"It's awkward being the only naked one, Sir. I want to see you."

Marcus shook his head then lay down next to me. He propped himself up on his elbow and cradled his head in his hand. He idly played with my nipples, tweaking first the right, then the left, my body shuddering under his touch.

"Not yet, Sweetness. Fuck, you look gorgeous tied to my bed. I've pictured this at least a dozen times already as I watch you begging me to let you come. I want you to focus on feeling instead of thinking. You're always inside your head. I need you out here with me."

He sat up, turning slightly as he reached for something behind him. As he turned back to me, I noticed a royal blue silk cloth in his hand. Before I guessed his intentions, he leaned toward me, placed the cloth over my eyes, and tied it behind my head.

"This will help you focus on my touch. Remember to let me know if your arms or legs start going numb, and I'll loosen the bonds. But for now, I want every part of you open for my exploration. Not a single inch of your body will go untouched tonight." He punctuated this by sliding his hands up my calves toward my core.

Without warning, hot, wet heat engulfed my breast. My back arched toward the source and a breath of air escaped my lips. "Oh God, Marcus."

A sharp pinch to my nipple had me flinching in pain.

"You will address me properly, sub."

"Sir, I'm sorry. I just need…"

He interrupted me. "You need what I tell you. Now be a good little sub and feel."

Marcus suckled my breasts again. My focus was entirely on the pulling of my nipples that I didn't realize his hand moved further up the length of my leg until a sharp pinch to my clitoris jerked me to attention. Immediately, two fingers were thrust into my pussy. My breath caught at the penetration.

"Yes," I hissed.

"You like that. But you need more don't you?" It wasn't a question. He continued pistoning his long fingers in and out of my wetness, this time adding a third finger.

Moans of pleasure poured from my throat. Tension spread, until out of nowhere, spasms raced through me as I reached my peak. My pussy tightened around Marcus' fingers. I don't know if I passed out, but my whole body was buzzing. I knew I was still bound to the bed. Other than that, my surroundings were foggy.

"I love watching you come," came the whisper from beside me. "And we're just getting started."

I heard a noise I didn't recognize.

"You're so hot, I think you need something to cool you off."

This was the only warning I received before a bite of cold spread across my lips. *So that's what the ice bucket was for.* Back and forth, he rubbed the ice as it slowly melted into my partially open mouth. I followed the water with my tongue and licked it up as it melted away. Marcus' hand left my mouth and a shiver ran down my spine as another ice cube rubbed across my nipple.

"Marcus…Sir," burst from my lips.

When I didn't think I could take the almost painful cold, the hot cavern of his mouth joined the ice cube and the combination surrounding my breast made me writhe in ecstasy. I heard more noise, and more ice was pressed to my throbbing clit.

"Fuck. Fuck. I can't take any more."

He ignored me as up and down, from slit to clit, ice was rubbed all over me. I struggled against the silk cords. Like my breasts, the heat of his mouth overlapped the cold of the ice. Added to the mix, Marcus nipped and sucked on my clit. Repeatedly, he alternated ice then heat until another powerful orgasm raced through me. I screamed his name as I arched off the mattress.

"You're so beautiful," he lovingly told me as I languished in his bed after the two most powerful orgasms I'd ever experienced. He controlled everything about my body, and I was powerless against him.

"God, the things I let you do to me," I gasped, still twitching from my release.

"Sweet, this is just the beginning," he laughed softly.

Groaning, I twisted in my bonds. Marcus first removed the blindfold and then unbound my arms and legs, checking them over.

"No numbness or tingling?"

I wiggled my fingers and toes. "No, Sir."

"Turn over."

Lazily, I complied, and he grabbed one of the large

cream pillows from the bed and stuffed it under my hips, effectively raising my ass in the air. I turned my head to the side and faced the mirror. I observed us as though we were two actors performing in a play. It just didn't feel real. I watched as Marcus slowly undressed. First, he removed his dress shirt, button by button, before tossing it over the arm of the midnight blue armchair next to the French doors that opened into the large master bath I'd recently exited. Muscles flexed in his arms and chest as he peeled the undershirt over his head, exposing the most amazing set of abs to ever grace a man's body.

I continued laying there, mesmerized by the strip show he was performing. He kicked off his shoes before slowly unbuckling his pants. He knew I was watching in anticipation. I loved his cock, and I was desperate to feel it again. It seemed like a lifetime ago since I'd felt him plunging into my depths.

In the blink of an eye, Marcus removed his pants, and they also met with the arm of the chair. It was impossible not to lick my lips as I took in his glorious length. His cock bobbed up and down as pre-cum leaked from its head. I wished he was close enough for me to lap up his essence. I watched his reflection through the mirror as he climbed up and straddled my backside, his cock lying perfectly in the crease of my ass.

"What color are you?"

"So much green, Sir."

"Don't forget your safe word," he warned like I should be prepared for what was coming next.

He reached over me and into the same bedside table that had contained the cords he had used to tie me and pulled out a small jar. He opened the jar, and scents of bergamot, coriander, and orange filled the room. Marcus dipped his fingers inside and when he pulled them out, they glistened.

Starting at my shoulders, he began a deep, sensuous massage, kneading the knots in my muscles. I closed my eyes as I relaxed under his expert touch. He released the tightness by drawing big circles up and down my back and rubbing certain spots. For what seemed like hours, he continued the massage before shifting himself further down the bed until he started up again.

Marcus massaged my feet, not forgetting my toes, before moving up to my calves and then my thighs. He continued massaging my thighs, which I widened almost unconsciously, and before I took my next breath, his finger pushed deep into my dripping core from behind. I pressed up coaxing him to go deeper. I gasped when he smacked my ass.

"Don't move."

He thrust in and out and wetness poured from my pussy. Before I could guess his intent, he slowly dragged his finger up and lightly massaged my anus, using both my own moisture and the oil to coat the ring. I squeezed my cheeks almost instinctively against the invasion.

"Relax, Sweet. I'm going to make you feel so good. Just keep breathing."

I forced myself to follow Marcus' instruction. For years, I'd been fascinating by anal sex and even though I'd experimented a little, it was different experiencing the sensation caused by someone else.

"You need to loosen up if I'm going to get a plug in there. I'll try to take it as slow as I can, but know that I can't wait to drive my cock in there, watching as I stretch this hole wide."

I shivered as I pictured his cock thrusting into my ass. He continued rubbing circles around my ring which loosened little by little with each one he made until I was relaxed enough that he slid his finger all the way in. He thrust inside my hole several times, which had me panting at the intrusion. When he removed the digit, my anus clamped down on emptiness.

I felt more oil being poured over my ass and dripping down my crack. Marcus' fingers returned to my asshole, only this time, it entered with more ease.

"I want you to inhale. As you exhale, push out."

At my exhale, I pushed out as Marcus had instructed and I felt a slight burn and stretch as he added another finger. In and out, he pressed and added in a scissoring pattern to open me up wider. I don't remember him getting into the nightstand again after picking up the oil, but he must have, because suddenly his fingers were gone and replaced by something much bigger.

"God, I can't wait until it's my cock inside you instead."

I struggled to catch my breath as I felt the pressure of the plug against my ass.

"Breathe in, and then as you breathe out, try to push the plug out."

Taking a deep breath in, I concentrated on relaxing as I exhaled and pushed out at the same time. Even before I'd completed my inhale, the plug was being gently pushed into my ass. I forced myself to relax when I was stretched wider than I ever thought possible as Marcus slid it the rest of the way in. I winced at the stronger pinch of pain as the flared base added that final, additional stretch before the plug was fully seated in my ass.

"Oh my God, I'm so full."

I lay there trying to catch my breath as the sensation of having something in my ass washed over me. It was mildly uncomfortable and foreign. I wanted to experience everything so I continued to force myself to relax. Before I knew it, the intense pressure had eased, and I slowly grew accustomed to the full sensation.

"Fucking gorgeous. Seeing you with a plug and knowing that soon it'll be my cock there instead has me almost ready to blow. Get ready to have both holes filled. Only imagine it's two cocks. Two mouths. Two sets of hands doing nothing but pleasing you."

My body quivered at the thought. I remembered the man at Eden, Donovan, and his allusion to a threesome. Suddenly, that was all I could think about. Damn Marcus for putting that in my head.

"Oh, you like that idea don't you? I can tell—you clamped down on the plug. You want it all. Jesus, you're killing me. I don't think I can go easy on you right now. I need to fuck you, and I need to fuck you hard."

I heard the condom wrapper and then Marcus grabbed my hips, lined his cock up to my cunt and thrust all the way to the hilt. I screamed in pleasure at the sensation of being filled. With the plug in my ass, the fit inside my pussy was as tight as a glove. Ruthlessly, he fucked me. With each thrust of his cock, the silicone pushed further inside my ass and the dual sensation of being filled in both holes was more than I could take, especially after the two orgasms I'd already had.

Boldness came over me just then. I reached down

between my legs and played with my clit. I was desperate for release and with a few flicks, I screamed out my climax at the same time I heard the roar of pleasure as Marcus echoed my release. Collapsing on the bed, I was lost to the world. I barely felt Marcus pull me up against him, his cock and the plug still inside me.

CHAPTER 18

I WOKE to the feel of fingers lightly caressing my chest. Opening my eyes, I peered down to see bright blue ones looking back at me.

"Good morning."

"Well, good morning to you as well. How are you feeling this morning?"

Penny beamed up at me. "Wonderful. A little achey, but in a tingly way."

"You were beautiful last night." I linked our fingers and brushed a kiss across them.

"You made me feel beautiful. Thank you for everything."

"Always a pleasure."

Her gaze traveled downward and her fingers followed. I sucked in a breath when they danced across my stomach, pausing just above the sheet. My cock twitched in response.

"Don't mind him. He just appreciates the lustful gaze of a voluptuous goddess such as you."

Giggling, she raised her eyes to meet mine. "So, you're saying I should ignore him and he'll go away? I don't want to be rude and not offer a proper good morning."

Even before Penny finished her sentence, her hand made its way under the covers to grasp my cock. Simultaneously sitting up and elbowing the sheet out of the way, she peppered kisses down my chest giving a little nip here and there, her gaze never once leaving mine. Her hand started an almost timid stroking motion. My muscles tightened when she circled my belly button with her tongue and then followed the narrow line of hair down.

Leisurely, she ran her tongue up the underside of my cock before giving it a little swirl around the head. She licked down my length again before gently sucking on first one ball sac then the other, her hand returning to stroking. She tempted and teased me with varying strokes and licks until at last she took me fully into her mouth.

Penny hollowed her cheeks and continued fucking her mouth and hand with my cock. I wanted to feel her entire throat milking me.

"Take a deep breath and relax your throat," I instructed.

Inhaling deeply, she did her best to relax her throat and continued lowering her head while moving her hand out of the way. Finally, the head of my cock hit the back of her throat, and she gagged and coughed, forcing her to pull back.

"Gently," I coaxed in a husky, arousal-filled tone.

Recovering quickly, she tried again, this time taking me a little farther each time until she'd almost swallowed my entire length. Up and down her mouth moved over me until I could feel my balls tightening. I wasn't going to last much longer.

"I want you to swallow everything I give you. Can you do that for me, Sweet?" I choked out knowing my release was imminent.

Penny hummed her agreement and that small vibration was all it took. Before I knew it, my seed exploded from me and washed the back of her throat. She continued swallowing until she'd taken every last drop I'd given her. With a pop, she pulled her lips away from my still semi-hard cock licking her lips as she went.

"Well, damn. That was certainly worth waking up to."

She collapsed onto the bed next to me with a satisfied sigh. I rolled onto my side and leaned down for a kiss, tasting myself on her lips.

"I'm going to take a shower quick. Feel free to join me if you'd like. Then I'm heading down to make us some breakfast. Afterwards, I need to run into my office to get some work done. How about dinner tonight?"

"Sounds lovely," she sighed dreamily.

I'D FINISHED up at the office a little earlier than I'd expected, so when I passed the florist shop on the way to pick up Penny, I pulled in. Fifteen minutes later I was back in my car, the single red rose filling my car with its lovely scent. When I parked in front of Penny's house, I grabbed the flower and headed to her door.

"Oh, Marcus," she exclaimed when she spotted me holding the bloom. "It's lovely. Thank you."

I handed her the rose and dropped a soft kiss on her

lips, lingering long enough to make her want more before I pulled away. "Not nearly as lovely as you."

She ducked her head in response and smiled softly. "Thank you for both the compliment and the beautiful flower. I love it. Let me put this in some water and then I'll be ready."

She hurried to the kitchen and back. I turned at her approach and held out my hand. "Shall we?"

Placing her hand in my outstretched one, she nodded. "Yes, Sir."

I continued holding her hand as we drove. At Fratello's, we were greeted by the maître d' who sat us at a booth in a corner at the back of the restaurant.

"After you." I gestured for her to slide in first and then I followed behind.

Our waiter came and took our drink orders before heading into the kitchen. Needing to feel her skin against mine, I clasped her hand again, rubbing my thumb over her knuckles. I didn't think I'd ever get bored touching her.

"I don't think I told you how beautiful you look tonight. I love that dress on you."

Penny smiled at the compliment. "Thank you."

I released my hold on her and moved my arm under the table to place my hand on her thigh instead. Her lips parted on a silent sound.

"Leave your hands where they are," I ordered when she made to move them.

Cotton caught against my calloused fingers as I walked them along her thigh, pulling the fabric upward with each bend of my knuckles. Penny's eyes darkened in arousal and she shifted nervously as her thighs were exposed to the cold restaurant air.

"Marcus?" My name came out breathy.

I responded with an innocent smile at the same time I slid my hand between her legs, gently nudging her to separate them farther. Her gaze darted between mine and the other occupants of the restaurant, but she complied. I pushed my advantage and traced her silk-covered slit, feeling the fabric grow damp with her juices.

"You like being naughty don't you? Wondering if any of these people knows what I'm doing to you over here. Do you think they can tell I'm rubbing your sweet pussy and how much you love it? Don't deny it either, because I can feel your cream through your panties."

Her breaths came in short pants. "Yes, Sir."

"There's a small problem though." I mockingly scolded. "I don't want anything separating my finger and your wet cunt. I want you to take them off."

She swallowed hard. "Okay."

When she scooted toward me, I shifted my hand and gripped her thigh, effectively stopping her.

"Where do you think you're going?" I growled.

Her gaze nervously darted around the restaurant. "I was going to the restroom to take them off as you requested, Sir."

I stared at her expectantly. "I want you to take them off right here, right now. Lift your butt up, slide them down your legs, and hand them to me."

Penny scanned the room again and panicked a little when she spied the waiter heading our way.

"Sir, can I please wait until the waiter leaves?"

I paused as though considering her request. "No, I don't think so."

She heaved a sigh and as inconspicuously as possible, she inched her dress up a little and wiggled her underwear down. The waiter reached our table and asked if we were ready to order. I ordered chicken parmesan with a side salad and Penny parroted my order, most likely in hopes the waiter disappeared quickly.

"I'll have the same thing he's having."

I couldn't help but chuckle. And prolong her agony.

I stopped the waiter's retreat. "Excuse me, but could you tell me what wine you would recommend to go with our meal?"

She groaned in frustration next to me. I merely quirked an eyebrow and cleared my throat to signify my impatience. I saw the waiter's eyes dance in Penny's direction during his recitation of wines. As I pondered which one to order, she continued sliding her underwear down her legs. She shifted to the side slightly and then reached under the table. I felt the hard nudge to my leg letting me know she was passing them off to me.

I made a huge production of taking them from her hand as I leaned sideways to stuff them in my pants pocket.

"I think we'll take a bottle of your finest Merlot."

The waiter's eyes widened, and the biggest smile spread across his lips. He quickly glanced at Penny again before answering, "I'll bring that right out, sir. Ma'am."

He inclined his head in her direction before strutting off to the kitchen where I was sure he'd tell the entire kitchen staff about the woman taking her underwear off under the table.

I couldn't help but laugh when she jabbed me in the side with her elbow.

"That was the most embarrassing thing that has ever happened to me. You know he's telling everyone what I was doing over here. Honestly, I'm surprised you didn't sniff them before you put them in your pocket," she huffed.

At that, I threw my head back, laughing loudly enough to attract the attention of several other patrons, who turned their head at the noise. When I finally finished laughing I was wiping tears from my eyes.

"Oh, Sweetness, don't give me any ideas."

When Penny tried to tug her dress back down, I stayed her with my hand on her leg again. "Keep it pulled up. I want to see you."

She froze.

"Tell me about your day. Did you do anything exciting after you left the house this morning?" I drew lazy designs across the top of her thigh.

She shrugged. "Not really. Ran a few errands and read a little. I even got a short nap in."

"That's good. Hopefully that means you'll have plenty of energy tonight."

I shifted my touch and her breath quickened. The circles I'd been drawing on her thigh were now being drawn around her clit. Slow, then fast. Soft, then hard. I continued my assault to her senses even as the waiter returned with our wine.

My finger slipped lower, teasing her opening, causing Penny to shift in her seat. A soft moan escaped before she could stop it, and the waiter paused pouring the wine to look at her. She forced herself to stop moving and offered a bored smile. Clearly, her acting skills needed work because he winked at her. Her whole face flushed bright red.

Finally, the waiter left us alone just as I slid my entire finger into her pussy and crooked it upward. Her hands flattened onto the top of the table until her fingertips turned white and her whole body was tense and ready for release. I withdrew my single digit until only the tip was touching her before plunging it back in. On and on I fucked her with my hand occasionally stopping, only to press it in deeper and to scrape across her g-spot again until wetness coated her thighs and no doubt the booth seat below her.

I spotted the waiter returning, and just as he stepped up to the table to deliver our food, I drove two fingers into her wet pussy, causing a roaring orgasm to rush through her. Her nails dug into the wood of the table as she restrained herself from moving and screaming out her release. Shivers continued to rack her body as she ducked her head to calm her breathing. I had no doubt she witnessed the bulge in my pants. I hope she took comfort in the fact that I was in pain with the lack of my own climax. She didn't look up until the waiter had gone.

When her gaze met mine, I could only imagine what she saw reflected back at her. I hoped she saw the pride, awe, and a more intent emotion I wasn't sure I could hide.

"That was the most beautiful thing I've ever witnessed. Watching you lose control like that was spectacular. You are beautiful and sexy, and everyone here is going to see how much you turned me on when we get up to leave, because I don't see myself losing this erection any time soon. I'm going to have a hard-on for days."

Some of her embarrassment left at my words. "Good. You deserve it for what you just did to me."

I nodded. "You're probably right."

We spent the rest of the evening enjoying our meal and talking about anything and everything. I'd never felt closer to another woman before. When I dropped her off, she invited me inside. Reluctantly, I declined. I needed to meet with Connor. Instead, I left her with a kiss and a promise to call tomorrow.

CHAPTER 19

"I CAN'T BELIEVE I let you talk me into going to yoga last week," Bridget whined while I sat on the edge of my bed watching her dig through my clothes.

I laughed when she full-body shuddered and her lips puckered like she'd sucked on a bad lemon. She and I had hit up my weekly, early Wednesday morning class. I'd been taking yoga for years, and it was the one thing I anticipated every week. Even though I was a big girl, it made me feel powerful and healthy. I maintained advanced level poses longer and with better technique than women ten years younger and fifty pounds lighter than me. I knew I shouldn't compare myself to others, but it still made me feel better about myself knowing the things my body did. Things younger, skinnier bodies, like Bridget, had difficulty with.

My yogi, Esther, was seventy if she was a day, and I wanted to be as healthy and bad ass as she was when I reached her age. We'd taken a couple spots right in the front of the class and started with a light warm-up. Forty-five sweaty minutes later, Bridget hadn't stopped bitching. I only laughed.

"I can't help it you're out of shape."

"If taking a damn contortionist class constitutes getting into shape, then fuck you very much. I'll stick with getting my exercise at Eden."

I rolled my eyes.

"Since I was forced to go to that horrid class with you, it's payback time. Today, you and I are going shopping. It'll be fun."

Now it was my turn to cringe.

"You need more sexy clothes," she stated as she rifled through my closet.

"Why do I need more sexy clothes? Marcus doesn't care what I wear. In fact, if it were up to him I'd show up to Eden naked. I hate shopping anyway, as you well know, so spending time going from store to store is not exactly what I would describe as fun. I can never find anything that fits right. So, excuse me if I'm not as excited about the prospect as you are."

"Well, I love shopping, so I'll be excited enough for both of us. Now, come on. Humor me. We're going to find you some sexy ass outfits that you'll thank me for later."

I groaned but let Bridget drag me off to wherever it was she was taking me.

Three hours later, I swore to God that I would never let Bridget talk me into shopping with her ever again. I'd rather be bound and tortured, and not in the sexy and fun way, before I ever put myself through this again. It was fucking exhausting. I didn't even know there were that many lingerie stores in town. She cooed and squealed at every other outfit I tried on. She even tried to take pictures to send to Marcus, but I put my foot down at that. I trudged behind her from the last store toward her car with her chattering like a magpie. I didn't pay attention to my surroundings. Not even when I heard the squeal of tires.

"Penny!" Bridget screamed.

I looked up as a flash of silver headed straight toward me. I barely had time to jump out of the way before the front bumper of the car skimmed against my hip, knocking me to the ground.

I lay there for a minute, breathless, hearing Bridget scream my name. I was so intent on catching air, I only gasped as she dropped to her knees next to me, looking around for help.

"Holy fuck, Penny, talk to me. Are you hurt? Oh my God, someone help us."

Finally, air entered my lungs, and I rolled to my side, gasping and coughing. I waved her off as I gingerly made my way to my feet, limping slightly at the discomfort in my hip and still trying to take in a full breath of oxygen.

"Miss Stephens, are you okay?"

I glanced to my left to see a well-dressed man standing next to Bridget, a wireless Bluetooth microphone in his ear. This must be one of my security detail. A fat lot of good he did me.

"I'm fine," I choked out. "A little shook up is all. What the hell was that?"

Bridget glared in the opposite direction. "That fucking car about ran you down is what. I wish I'd seen the license plate number. We need to call the police and Marcus."

Still slightly shaken up, it took me a minute to get my bearings.

The guard spoke up. "I've already contacted Mr. Black. He's on his way."

"I'm calling 9-1-1" Bridget already had her phone to her ear.

I spotted my purse on the ground where I'd landed and slowly bent down to pick it up. I guess it was up to me to call Marcus. I dug through it for my phone, dialed the number and paced, limping slightly, while I waited for him to answer.

"How was your shopping expedition with the the lovely Bridget?"

For a brief heartbeat, I didn't know where to start. "It was miserable, and I hated every second of it. It didn't get any better after someone just tried to mow me down with their car."

Silence reigned on the other end long enough for me to think the call had dropped.

"Marcus, are you still there?"

It was then I heard a laundry list of swear words, including some I'd never heard before, and the loud crash of breaking glass.

"Sir, talk to me. What's happening?" My nerves were already shot, and he wasn't helping any.

"Nothing, sorry, I dropped my glass. Are you okay? You're not hurt are you? I should have asked right away. And where's your goddamn security?" He sounded calm now. Eerily calm.

"They're here. Well, one of them is anyway. And no, I'm not hurt, other than my hip aching where the car grazed me. I'm mostly scared and shaken up. Other than that, I'm okay. Bridget called the police, and they're on their way. So's Connor."

"Where are you? I'm coming to get you."

I almost told him not to worry about it, but I realized I needed him here. Holding me.

"We're near the South parking garage downtown. The one on Courtland Street."

"Don't move from that spot," he ordered. "I'm on my way."

Intense relief filled me. "Yes, Sir. We'll be here."

CHAPTER 20

RAGE AND TERROR battled inside me as I raced to get to Penny. Evan was behind this. Connor and I were scheduled to pay a visit to one of the local precincts later today. One of his contacts at the force had made an arrest—a woman who confessed to being the one feeding Evan intel regarding the search for him. She was the reason he'd evaded Connor's team for so long. According to her, however, she didn't realize the type of person he was until it was too late. We'd been hoping to get a lead on his whereabouts when we went to speak to her today. Now, it was more important than ever that we talk to her.

I broke every speed limit on my drive downtown and it still felt like it was taking me forever to reach Penny's location. Finally, I turned the last corner, and there in front of me were several police cars as well as the paramedics. My heart dropped thinking she was more hurt than she'd let on. That is until I spotted her sitting on the tailgate of the ambulance. She appeared unharmed other than holding something against her hip. I threw the truck in park and dove out from behind the wheel.

"Penny!" I almost ran to where she sat.

Her head jerked up at my voice and I saw the relief on her face. As I closed the distance, I saw the tears form until her expression crumpled just as I reached her. She threw herself into my arms and I crushed her against me as she bawled against my chest. I spotted Connor and two men over the top of her head talking to a tall, sandy-brown haired officer who looked like he should be holding a surf-board instead of wearing a gun. I didn't see Bridget anywhere. When the men caught my eye, they excused themselves and made their way over.

"What the fuck happened?" I barked when they joined us.

"Bridget and Penny were walking back to Penny's car after leaving a store when a silver vehicle, possibly a Honda, attempted to run them down. Witnesses said they saw a single occupant inside. White male, possibly in his 30s or 40s, wearing a ball cap and sun glasses. Parker jumped out of the security vehicle to check on the women while Mills attempted to pursue the other car, but he was evaded."

Penny pulled back from me on a shuddery inhale, wiping her eyes, but my arm remained firmly around her waist keeping her close. She didn't fight my embrace, but instead wrapped her arms around me and rested her head against my shoulder.

"So, he got away." It wasn't a question.

Connor's expression was grave. "Yes. But Webber has the woman in custody and the plan in still to speak with her today. He says she can lead us to Evan."

"You'll have to go without me. I need to take Penny to the hospital."

The woman in question pushed back from me. "Marcus, I'm fine. The paramedics already checked me out. Nothing is broken. I just need some Tylenol, ice, and rest. Really. Finding Evan is more important. If this woman is the key, then you need to speak to her. Please, Sir."

I sighed at that last. "Fine, but I don't like this. Not one fucking bit. I'll take you home and get you settled with some pain meds and in bed. But the minute we're done with this woman, I'm coming back to your house. If you're not feeling better, you *will* go to the hospital. Is that clear?"

"Yes, Sir."

I turned back to look at Connor. "I'll meet you at the station in an hour."

I TURNED my head in the direction of my name being called. The same officer Connor had been speaking to at the scene stood outside a door.

"I'm Detective Webber. Come with me, please."

I followed him down a hallway where he opened a door and ushered me in. The room was dark and on one wall was a two-way mirror. I stepped over to it and through the glass I saw the female sitting alone at a table in the adjoining room.

"Connor had to step out, but he'll be back in a minute. The two of you can remain in here while I question Ms. Watson. I'm going against policy by having a civilian listen in on an interrogation. Don't make me regret it."

The detective turned and exited the room just as Connor arrived.

"Good, you're here. How's Penny?"

My jaw clenched. "Hurting. But, she'll be okay. Just needs to stay off that leg for a few days."

He laid his hand on my shoulder. "I'm sorry she was hurt, Marcus."

I nodded and he removed his hand.

Just then Webber entered the opposite room and sat across from Ms. Watson. Connor and I stepped closer to the glass.

"Can you tell me your full name, please?" the detective asked her.

"Maggie Watson."

"And Ms. Watson, can you please tell me your occupation?"

Her fingers twisted nervously on top of the table. "I'm a German-speaking contract interpreter for The Office of Language Services under the US Department of State."

Webber shifted some papers around and pulled out an eight by ten photo. He flipped it around to face her.

"Do you know this man?"

Instantly her eyes filled with tears. "Yes. His name is Evan Banks."

"Can you tell me about your relationship with Mr. Banks?" his question was gentle.

She wiped away a stray tear and sniffed. "We met about six months ago. I was at a work conference at a local hotel. I'd stopped by the bar for a drink and he introduced himself to me. Shortly after that, we started dating."

My fists clenched at my sides while I waited for the next question.

"What caused the relationship between you and Mr. Banks to end?"

I thought tears were going to start falling, but she managed to hold them back.

"He became verbally abusive. He made physical threats against my aging father if I didn't do what he told me to."

Webber pulled back the photo and shuffled the papers again. "And what did Mr. Banks tell you to do?"

Ms. Watson's shoulders straightened. "He told me that the only reason he approached me at the bar that night was because he'd discovered I was working on a case that gave me access to records at Black Light Security. That was when he threatened my father if I didn't try and find information regarding a Grace Hathaway."

"And did you provide Mr. Banks with this information?"

She shook her head. "No. I wasn't able to find anything related to her. The only thing I did send him was the home address of a Marcus Allen as well as a couple of appointments I overheard Mr. Black's secretary making. That was all."

Webber shifted in his chair and crossed one ankle over his knee. "If Mr. Banks threatened you or your family, why are you coming forward with this info?"

Now the tears began to fall in earnest. "My father passed away. Evan no longer has anything to hold over my head. I couldn't keep quiet any longer. Especially after he hit me. I knew then that I had to do something."

Webber pulled out a notepad and pen from his inner jacket pocket. "Can you tell me where to locate Mr. Banks?"

Ms. Watson wiped her eyes and nose. "The last time we spoke, a week ago, he was renting a room in a beach house out on Patterson Island. I can give you the address."

He scribbled the information she recited onto his notepad before rushing from his chair and pocketing it. "Thank you, Ms. Watson. I have more questions for you, but I'll give you a few moments."

Connor and I only waited briefly before he entered the room.

"So, now we have last known location. I'm going to send a patrol car over there and see if they can't find him."

"And then what?" I asked.

Webber shrugged. "If he's there, we'll arrest him. If not, we'll wait until he shows up. Either way, at least we have something. And if either of you attempt to approach the house I'll have you brought up on charges of hindering an investigation."

Connor tilted his head in the direction of the interrogation room. "What happens to her?"

"Unless we can prove that she had prior knowledge to Evan's crimes, then sadly, she's just as much of his victim as Grace. You can, of course, press charges for her illegal obtainment, and dispersement, of confidential information, but that's about it."

"I see. Well, thank you for letting us be here."

I wasn't entirely satisfied, but at least Evan was within reach. I turned to Connor.

"You guys figure out what needs to be done. I'm going to check on Penny. Keep me updated."

He inclined his head.

Without any goodbye, I left the station and drove home. I needed to touch her and make sure she was okay.

CHAPTER 21

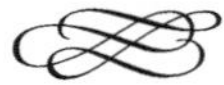

I ENDED up taking a short nap after Marcus left, but now I was awake and aching. I ran a bath and poured in some Epsom salt. When the tub was full and steam filled the room, I got undressed and slowly slid into the hot water, my hip slightly protesting the movement. I grabbed the rolled up towel I'd placed on the ledge of the garden tub, tucked it behind my head, and closed my eyes. I might have dozed off again, because my eyes popped open when I heard a noise.

"Penny?" Marcus quietly called from the living room.

"I'm in the tub," I hollered back.

There was a knock on the door and then it slowly swung open. He peeked around it.

"You can come in. I was just about to get out."

He stepped inside and grabbed the bath sheet off the rack for me.

"Let me help." I took his outstretched hand and he helped me stand before wrapping the towel around me.

"How you feeling, Sweet?"

I dried myself off. "Better. Just a little stiff, but the bath seems to have helped. How did it go at the police station?"

We exited the bathroom and Marcus sat on the edge of the bed while I threw on a pair of sleep shorts and shirt I was now thankful Bridget made me buy.

"We have Evan's last known address. Not sure if he's still there or not, but when I left, the police were heading that way to try and locate him. If he's there, they'll bring him in for questioning. The woman today said that he threatened her father's life if she didn't help him. So, they might get him for that. But based on the the kind of information she gave him, it probably isn't enough to put him away. There's also no way we can prove he was responsible for your accident today. Not unless someone can positively ID him as the one behind the wheel of the car that struck you."

"What about Connor? He doesn't have to play by the same rules the police does, right?" I pulled the shirt over my head, my voice muffled by my actions.

"Not really. He can put a tail on Evan. Of course, he'll play the victim and most likely file a complaint that he's being stalked. It's basically a no win situation, even now knowing where he is. Not until we can pin something on him."

"So, we're all pretty much in the same position we've been for weeks now." I sighed in disgust.

Marcus shrugged. "Basically."

My stomach chose that moment to rumble. He stood and reached for my hand. "Come on. Let's get you fed."

We headed through the living room, where Marcus paused to turn on the stereo. With soft music playing in the background, we worked together in the kitchen, putting together a delicious, easy meal of caesar salad, spaghetti, and garlic bread. I set the dining room table and lit the two candles in the middle for a soft, romantic glow to the room. We took the food dishes out and Marcus plated our meal as I took my seat.

We ate our meal in an unusual silence, both of our minds elsewhere. Sipping the Moscato I'd poured myself, I glanced over at him and noticed a far away look in his eye as he picked at his meal. The silence overpowered everything. I had to do something to break it. I reached over to clasp his calloused hand, squeezing Marcus' fingers.

"Thank you for being there for me today."

He squeezed them back but with a sad smile. "It's my fault you were hurt. I can't stop thinking that if not for me, this wouldn't have happened to you. I'm sorry, Penny."

I covered his hand with both of mine. "Stop. The only person to blame for this is Evan. You do such a great job taking care of me. That's what people in relationships do. They support each other with whatever is going on in their lives, and help them with any problems they're having."

Leaning over, Marcus pulled me out of my chair and into his lap. I snuggled closer, inhaling the familiar woodsy smell, and wrapped my arms around his muscular shoulders. His arms surrounded me, with one arm around my back and the other across the top of my thighs. His fingertips traced invisible patterns on my hip, where a giant bruise was beginning to show.

"I don't know what I'd do if I'd lost you." He tilted my chin up until our gazes met. "I'm falling in love with you."

An emotion unlike anything else I'd ever felt rushed through me.

"I love you too."

Marcus leaned down and our lips met for a different kind of kiss between us. This one spoke of tenderness. Joy. Love. Soon though, it turned heated.

Tongues tangled.

Breaths mingled.

Body temperatures rose.

He fisted my hair and tilted my head to deepen the connection. I writhed on his lap in arousal. I pulled back, panting with the need to pull air into my lungs.

"Make love to me, Sir," I murmured against his lips.

I rose from his lap and with only a slight tug on his hand, I pulled him to his feet. He leaned down to blow out the candles before letting me lead him back to his bedroom. I stood at the foot of the bed and slowly undressed him. I ran my hands up his rock-hard abs and chest exposing inch by glorious inch as I raised his shirt up and over his head. I tossed it off to the side and then dropped to my knees. My hip protested a little.

"Penny," Marcus growled a warning.

I tilted my head back and begged him with my eyes. "I'm all right, Sir. I swear."

Ignoring any further attempts to stop me, I carefully undid his pants and lowered them to his ankles as he raised one foot after the other to step out of them. I reached my hand out to clasp the cock that had sprung free of his pants and now stood at attention. With a quick swipe of my tongue, I laved the end, before sucking the full length deep into my mouth. I pulled back a little before taking him in deep again. I'd just started enjoying myself when Marcus groaned.

"Stop," he ordered and gently pulled me to my feet.

I sent him a mock pout. "But Sir, I wasn't done."

"If you kept going, this would be over before it even began. Now, be quiet and let me return the favor." He slipped my shirt over my head and tugged my shorts down, taking care with my hip. I was about to burst and he prolonged my agony by taking his time. I knew though not to rush him. He would go at his own pace and not a second faster, no matter how much I begged and pleaded. I accepted that he controlled things right now.

He brushed my collarbones with his fingertips. My nipples pebbled in the cool air as his heated gaze skimmed my breasts.

"You are so beautiful, Penny. I don't ever want you to forget that. No matter what, I want you to know that you are a strong, gorgeous woman who deserves only the best in your life."

"You make me feel beautiful, Sir. Never before has anyone done for me what you have. You've given me everything I ever needed. More than I ever dreamed. You make me a stronger person. I love you, Marcus."

I stared into his green eyes and knew beyond a shadow of doubt that my love was returned.

"I love you too."

He threaded his fingers through my hair, wrapping his other arm around my waist, and pulled me flush against him. He looked into my eyes for a second longer and then lowered his face to mine to place the gentlest of kisses on my lips. He continued kissing me before moving up to my nose and then my eyes as they fluttered shut. He rained soft kisses over my face before returning to my lips where he deepened the touch.

He broke away and helped me step out of the puddle

of clothing before leading me to the bed. There, Marcus worshipped my body with his touch as he traced his fingertips down my arms to my fingers and back up again. He made his way to my breasts before giving each nipple a slight pinch to increase the pleasure. He followed my breast bone down the middle of my chest, over my belly, and stopped right before he reached the place that ached for him. I closed my eyes as I reveled in his touch.

"Sir, please," I begged.

I needed him tonight more than ever. I could have been killed today, and I didn't want to waste one second of my life. When he didn't say anything, I peered up at him. His hand shifted to the bruise on my hip as his eyes followed suit.

"I'm so sorry you were hurt. I'm sorry I didn't protect you. I won't let it happen again."

I cupped his strong jaw on my palm. "Stop blaming yourself. Do you understand? It wasn't your fault. Now, I don't want to think about it anymore. I have far more important things on my mind."

I brought Marcus' head down to me and poured all my emotions into the kiss, transferring my love to him. When I tried to deepen the kiss, he pulled back a hair's breadth.

"There's no need to rush, Sweetness. We have all night."

He gentled the kiss, tasting every inch of my mouth, softly, sweetly. We kissed for what seemed like hours as he softly caressed my side, his thumb resting just below my breast. He reached out to grasp my hand and brought my arm above my head where he interlaced our fingers. He moved on top of me, and I spread my legs wider to make room for him, never breaking our sensual kiss. He repeated the move with my other hand so both my arms were bound together above my head with our fingers were intertwined together.

He broke our kiss and stared straight into my eyes. No words spoken between us. With our gazes remaining locked, I felt him shift and his cock slid up and down my slit, becoming wet with my juice, until he reached my pussy. He slowly entered me with gentle ease, his eyes never leaving mine. Once he was fully imbedded, I wrapped my legs around his waist as he thrust, taking his time, pausing slightly when just the tip was touching me before pushing back in. With every thrust of his hips I counter thrusted, bringing us as close as two people could get. Every time our pelvises met, the friction increased on my clit.

We continued our dance, until the pressure that had been building exploded and a kaleidoscope of colors burst across my vision, but I refused to break eye contact. Within seconds of my orgasm rushing over me, I was awash with his seed as Marcus reached his climax right behind mine. On and on tiny tremors continued to rush through our bodies until finally my body relaxed.

I unlocked my legs from around Marcus, and he rolled to his back, taking me with him. I cuddled up next to him with my arm across his chest and my head on his shoulder. His heartbeat thudded against my hand where it rested on his chest, and I matched my breathing to his until our hearts beat in harmony.

"I just made love to you without a condom."

I glanced up to meet his worried gaze. "I know. I'm on the pill and haven't been with anyone in over five years."

"I get tested regularly and I always wear protection. This was a first for me."

"Don't worry about it. Everything's fine." I placed a kiss on his chin.

I sensed his relief. I cuddled closer and savored our connection until exhaustion overtook me and I drifted off.

CHAPTER 22

EXHAUSTED, I glanced at the clock. It was just after dinner. My mind drifted for a moment, and melancholy washed over me.

I needed to make a trip to the safe house.

I packed up the portfolios, shut down the computer, and turned out my office lights before heading to the parking garage. Soon, I was making the short trek to the suburbs. I always took great pains to make sure I wasn't followed whenever I came here. It was imperative that Evan didn't find this place. After parking down the block, I waited a few minutes and looked around at my surroundings to make sure I didn't see anything out of the ordinary. When nothing caught my eye, I exited the car and took off through a nearby alleyway, cutting through several yards and crisscrossing a couple streets, before I finally reached my destination.

I knocked on the back door of a small, yellow house with the cookie cutter Cape Cod design of every third house in the development. It was the reason I chose this location. All the houses looked alike. Little ornamentation to make it memorable. After several minutes, the curtain on the window of the door slid to the side and a man peered out. Immediately, he unlocked the door and ushered me inside the kitchen before shutting the door behind us.

"What are you doing here? Is everything okay?"

After taking a seat on one of the bar stools at the kitchen island, I looked over at the armed man who'd granted me entrance. "Everything's fine. I just needed to see her. I was careful, I swear. No one followed me. I made sure of it. How is she? Anything new?"

Miles crossed his arms over his chest, pulling at the holster around his shoulders and back. "Everything's been quiet here. Nothing out of the ordinary to report. I know she misses you, though."

Sadness rushed through me. "I miss her too. I wish I could visit more often, but it's not safe. You know what Evan would do if he found Grace."

He nodded in understanding. "I get it, and I know it's just as hard on you as it is her. I don't envy your situation at all."

"Is she upstairs?" I tipped my head in that direction.

"I think she just finished her bath."

"I guess I should go say hello then."

"Enjoy your visit."

"Thanks, Miles."

I rose from the stool and went in search of Grace. Heading upstairs, I heard a feminine voice coming from the end of the hall. Sitting up in the bed was a beautiful blonde woman, and snuggled up next to her with a book in hand was a miniature version of her. A little girl, around two years old.

I watched them for a moment. When I shifted my weight, I moved enough to cause the door to open further and the hinges to squeak. The woman jumped and pivoted in the direction of the door, immediately poised to flee. The little girl, who hadn't yet been conditioned to jump at noises that might mean danger, turned her head more slowly to see what had interrupted her story time. When she spied me standing there, she dove off the bed and raced toward me with her arms outstretched.

"Daddy!" she yelled as she launched herself into my arms. She peppered sweet kisses all over my face, giggling as my scruff tickled her cheeks.

"I've missed you so much, baby girl," I hugged her tightly, inhaling the familiar little girl smell as I glanced over her head at the woman swinging her legs over the side of the bed.

"Hello, Marcus," she said.

"Grace."

An uncomfortable silence reigned as we stood side by side with our daughter between us. Within a minute, Grace stepped away. "I'll let you two catch up. I'll be downstairs when you're done."

Then she left me alone with our daughter and her giggles as Hailey told me about her day.

AFTER READING Hailey another bedtime story I tucked her into bed, kissed her goodnight, and went downstairs to speak with Grace. I found her curled up on the couch with a cup of the hot tea she loved. I made my way to the recliner next to the couch and took a seat.

"It's good to see you again. Have you been doing okay?"

She took a sip of her tea before answering, as if measuring her words. "You know how it is, Marcus. The same thing day in and day out. I'm slowly losing my mind."

"Grace—"

She held up her hand to interrupt me. "Stop. I've been living this life for three years. I get it. Everything you've done is for Hailey's and my safety, but I hate being in this house all the time. You have no idea how hard it is to keep a two-and-a-half-year-old entertained day in and day out, do you? Of course you don't, because you're never here."

I flinched guiltily because she was right.

She continued bitterly. "You're not the one who has to come up with creative ideas for a little girl to stay busy all the time. Or the one who has to comfort your daughter when she cries because her daddy leaves all the time. You're not the one stuck in a house alone, except for a toddler and an endless rotation of men who are paid to protect you, but not, apparently, to talk to you. I'm so lonely. If it weren't for Hailey, I'd rather take my chances with Evan. No matter how crazy my ex-husband is, at least there wasn't this endless sameness. I never knew what would set him off so at least it kept life interesting, even if I had bruises to go with it. I'm going insane here, Marcus. "

"Grace, I know this isn't ideal, and I'm sorry you're the one stuck in this horrible situation. Connor has a lead on

Evan. We're closer than ever to finding him. Once we do, this will all be over and you'll be safe."

Grace walked into the kitchen to place her teacup in the sink leaving me no choice but to follow. She sighed, wearily, as she leaned against the counter. Miles made his exit when we walked in so we were alone in the kitchen.

"Look, I'm sorry I snapped at you. I'm tired, although that's no excuse. I know you're doing everything you can. But for God's sake, Marcus, we've been here over two years. This isn't getting any easier. What about when Hailey needs to start school? What about friends? She can't stay in this house forever. I wish this were all over. God, I hate Evan. Marrying him was the second worse decision I've ever made."

The question popped out of my mouth before I could stop it. "What was the first worse decision you'd ever made?"

She stared me right in the eye. "When I broke it off with you all those years ago. We were so good together, you and me. I miss those days. I miss you."

I shifted awkwardly and looked at my feet.

Neither of us spoke for a minute.

I broke the uncomfortable silence between us. "I'm seeing someone."

"What's her name?" she asked quietly.

"Penny. She reminds me of you a little. Or at least the younger you. Innocent and a little naive." I hated hurting her this way.

"Do you love her?"

"Yes."

"She's an extremely lucky woman then."

Grace reached out to hug me. We were better off as

friends than lovers. We would always share our daughter, but our intimate relationship had been over for a long time. I hugged her back and kissed her on the cheek.

"I'm sorry, but I need to get going. Kiss our Hailey girl for me, and tell her I love her always."

CHAPTER 23

I GLANCED at the clock while I ignored my tired feet. I should have left an hour ago, but I'd picked up a couple extra hours for a co-worker who needed to come in late. I'd had some downtime about thirty minutes ago and texted Marcus to let him know I was going to be late, but a quick peek at my phone showed he hadn't responded yet. I sent up a small prayer that the evening remained quiet until I got off, however, from the sounds of it, I wasn't going to be so lucky.

From across the room, I could hear the charge nurse relaying information from telemetry about an incoming MVA, motor vehicle accident. The victim, a 40-year-old white male, was in critical condition. They rattled off the victim's vital signs while I listened in. *Crap*. I didn't expect I'd be leaving anytime soon.

I quickly headed to the open trauma bay where the rest of the team was already scrubbing in. I rushed to catch up and before I knew it, the triage team was pushing the stretcher into the bay with us. Everything was moving so fast, and I was in the zone, so I barely paid attention to the man on the table. We went to work stitching up the head wound. When I reached out to wash some of the blood from his face, I stumbled backward.

"Penny, are you all right?" One of my nurse co-workers asked.

The words froze in my throat and I couldn't respond. My vision grew blurry, and I vaguely heard one of the docs yell, "Get her out of here. Now."

Someone took my arm and pulled me blindly out of the room. There was a buzzing sound in my ears and my head was spinning a little.

"Here, take this and sit down."

I plopped into a chair the same time a wet object was thrust into my fingers. I brought the alcohol swab up to my nose and took a big sniff. The spinning slowed and the buzzing inside my head calmed. I looked up to see Rita, the charge nurse, standing over me.

"Feeling better?"

"Oh my god. That's my boyfriend. I need to get in there." I jumped to my feet to make my way back into the trauma room.

Rita blocked my way. "No, way. I can't let you back in there, Penny."

I pleaded with her, but she merely shook her head. "Can't do it. You head out to the waiting room, call your friends, and wait there. I'll see what I can find out and keep you updated. But I'm *not* letting you back in that room. You hear?"

Numbly, I nodded and made my way to my locker and grabbed my things. Then I headed out to the waiting room where, believe it or not, I'd never actually been. I'd always been on the other side of these walls. I called Bridget and burst into tears. Once I finally got out what happened, she told me she was already out the door. Within twenty minutes, she arrived.

"Holy shit, babe, are you okay? Have you heard anything? How's he doing?" Bridget pulled me into a giant hug and peppered me with questions.

"I don't know. My friend Rita is supposed to update me, but she hasn't been out here yet. He looked terrible, Bridget. Blood was everywhere. I know he has some type of head wound, but I don't know about any other injuries. I'm so fucking scared and worried and nervous all at once. I know the team that is working on him is doing the best they can. Honestly, it's probably better that I'm not in there. I couldn't focus knowing that Marcus was the patient I was working on."

I sank into the waiting room chair next to Bridget, beyond exhausted. Time dragged on until Rita finally showed up, and the expression on her face spoke volumes.

"He appears to have a head injury, which is what is concerning them the most. It's possible that his head hit the windshield, and they're worried about internal bleeding. Radiology has been notified, and once he's stabilized, they'll know the extent of the damage. He also has a broken leg and some internal injuries. That's all I have for you, Penny, I'm sorry."

"Thank you, Rita. I appreciate it more than you know." I fought the tears building, blinking rapidly to keep them from falling. I needed to be strong right now. Marcus had always been the strong one in our relationship. Now, it was my turn.

Bridget leaned over and hugged me close, "Oh, sweetie, I'm so sorry."

Resting my head on her shoulder, we continued to sit and wait for any news. I don't know how long we sat huddled next to each other, but exhaustion took over and my eyes grew heavy. I was jarred awake by someone nudging my shoulder. For a moment, I forgot where I was. Until I saw Rita standing over me and Bridget seated next to me.

"How long was I asleep? Any change? How's he doing? Is he going to be okay?" I felt Bridget stirring.

Rita placed both hands up palm facing toward me. "Calm down. He's going to be okay. They placed a few pins to set his leg and his spleen was removed. He's been moved to the ICU for monitoring. All scans show he is lucky and only has a severe concussion. He's not awake yet, so I can only let you see him for a few minutes if you want."

Tears of relief slid down my face with the news, and I felt Bridget's arms around me as the first sob escaped. I covered my face with my hands and sobbed uncontrollably. Finally, they slowed to a hiccup or two, and I quickly dried my eyes.

"I'll be back soon."

Bridget nodded, and I followed Rita through the halls.

"Just a few minutes," she reminded me when we stopped in front of a door.

I nodded while I gathered my courage. Then I walked in. On the bed in front of me lay Marcus, tubes and lines running everywhere, the beeping and whirring of the monitors the only sound in the room. I stepped up to the bed and reached out to hold his hand. It was surprisingly warm to the touch. Even under the gauze wrapped around his head, I noticed they'd shaved off part of his beautiful, dark wavy hair. I almost cried for its loss, which was ridiculous considering everything else.

Not wanting to disturb him, I leaned over and gently kissed his forehead and then brushed a soft kiss on his lips. I thought I felt a light squeeze of his hand on mine. I wasn't sure if it was real or wishful thinking. Knowing Rita was already risking a lot by letting me in here, I didn't stay any longer. I stepped outside and gave her a hug.

"Thank you for letting me see him."

"You're welcome. Now, go home and get some rest."

I nodded and made my way back out to where Bridget waited. Just as I stepped into the waiting room, my phone rang.

"Penny?" The deep male voice seemed frantic.

"Yes."

"Penny, it's Connor. Is Marcus with you?" The question sounded desperate.

He was making me nervous. "Sort of. He was in a car accident tonight, and I was on shift when they brought him in. Bridget's here with me now. They just took him to ICU. Why? What's wrong?"

"Fuck." I heard him curse in the background.

"Connor, damn it, what's going on?"

"Grace is dead."

All the air was sucked out of me. "Wha—What? When? How?"

Bridget was on full alert next me and whispered, "What's going on?"

"I need you to come to the safe house. I'll text you the address."

"Why?" I was so confused.

He sighed. "I'll tell you when you get here. Please. I need you here. Bring Bridget."

Still in shock, I agreed. "We're on our way."

"Just let them know Detective Webber and I called you here."

Connor disconnected the call.

"We have to go to the safe house. He said Grace is dead."

Bridget's eyes widened and her mouth dropped. "Oh, fuck. Hailey."

"Who's Hailey?"

She grabbed my hands in hers and squeezed them. "She's Marcus and Grace's daughter."

Within forty minutes, Bridget and I turned down Coach Street, where flashing lights lit up the night sky. On the street, in front of the safe house, were police cars and other emergency vehicles. The whole scene was surreal. I had to park two houses down and walk up the sidewalk toward the house. We hadn't even made it to the driveway when we were stopped by a police officer.

"I'm sorry, but this is a police crime scene. You can't be here."

Bridget put her hands on her hips.

"I'm afraid that's where you're wrong, Officer"—she squinted at his name tag—"Perkins. We're here to see Detective Webber or Connor Black."

"Penny? Bridget?"

We looked up at our names being called to see Connor standing outside the front door.

Bridget harrumphed and took off toward him. My brain still wasn't processing everything, so I was glad she was here to take the lead. I followed behind as the three of us ducked under the crime scene tape and entered the house. A quick survey of the living room showed complete disarray. Overturned furniture. Broken glass everywhere. Luckily, there were no signs of a body. We walked farther into the house and up a set of stairs into a room at the end of the hall.

Connor directed us to the chairs. "Have a seat please. I'll be right back."

Bridget took a seat, but I was too keyed up. All I could do was pace. I didn't know how long we waited, but there was a metallic click and the door opened again. I turned to see who it was and almost fainted. There stood Connor and this time he wasn't alone. In his arms was a little girl about two years old with the blondest hair and bright blue eyes sucking her thumb, her head resting against his shoulder.

"This is Hailey," he whispered.

My fingers went to my mouth to stop the sob from escaping. She was absolutely beautiful. I barely felt myself move, but the next thing I know I was standing right in front of them.

"Hi there," I breathed out, wanting to touch her so bad, but afraid to.

My eyes darted up to his. "May I hold her?"

Gently, in case she put up a fuss, I took Hailey out of his hands and pulled her against my chest. She sighed and snuggled close. At that exact moment, I fell in love.

CHAPTER 24

I STRUGGLED to open my eyes, almost like they were glued shut. I shifted, then winced at the movement when waves of agony shot through my entire body. I took inventory of each ache and pain, and didn't know which hurt worse, my leg or my head. I shook my head to get the kinks out and orient myself, but the torture of it made me stop. Finally, my eyes opened and then squeezed shut against the bright fluorescent lighting glaring down at me. I blinked several times and finally adjusted to the light.

As everything came into focus, I took in all the tubes in my body and the medical equipment lining the walls and realized I lay in a hospital bed. I took a chance against the pain and turned my head to peer at the room around me. Slouched in an awkward position in an extremely uncomfortable looking chair was Connor. Suddenly, the door opened and a nurse walked in.

"I'm sorry if I woke you up," she apologized.

"No, you're fine, I was awake. What happened? How

did I wind up here?" I cleared my throat when my voice came out a croak.

She didn't say anything at first as she walked over to check the monitors. "Are you in any pain?"

"Only when I move," I groaned.

"Understandable. Do you remember anything?"

Not wanting a repeat of the agony when I tried moving my head, I kept myself still. "I remember leaving a… friend's house. After that the rest is blank."

She offered me a sympathetic smile. "You were in a car accident. You have a concussion, a broken leg, and a few other various injuries. Let me go get the doctor, and he can speak to you. Press your call light next to the bed if you need anything."

The nurse vacated the room before I could ask anymore questions. I laid there for a while trying to stay awake, but it was becoming more difficult. I must have dozed, because when I next opened my eyes, Connor was there and watching me.

"Man, you look like shit."

I burst out laughing and then instantly regretted it. "Thanks a lot asshole. Jesus, everything hurts. It's like I was hit by a truck."

"You were."

I stopped laughing at his tone.

"What the hell happened?"

He paused too long.

"Connor? What the fuck is going on?"

He ran his hands through his hair with a sigh. "Were you at Grace's last night?"

"Yes. I left and —. That's the last thing I remember. Why?"

"Because we think Evan followed you."

I shot up in bed despite the pain. "What? No, I'm always careful."

His expression turned so grave, my heart dropped in my chest. "Connor?"

"Grace is dead," he blurted out. "So is Evan."

I could feel all the blood leaving my face.

"Hailey?" I croaked out.

"She's fine. Actually"—he paused like he wasn't sure what my response would be—"Penny is watching her."

As I began to speak, the nurse and doctor walked in. They examined me and asked me a series of questions, while Connor remained unobtrusive in the background and listened. The doctor recommended I remain in the hospital for a few more days for observation and after their brief conversation both the doctor and the nurse left us alone.

"How did it happen?"

He scooted to the edge of the chair and leaned forward balancing his elbows on his knees. "Apparently Evan snuck into the backyard. When the guards, Bradford and Willis, went to investigate, he shot them. He entered the premises and, from what we can tell, there was an argument and a physical altercation between him and Grace. Bradford survived the shooting and stumbled into the house to see them wrestling for control of the gun. He drew his sidearm, told Evan to drop the weapon, but was afraid to shoot for fear of hitting Grace. The weapon went off, and she was hit. When Evan turned on the guard, Bradford shot him multiple times in the chest. He then called 9-1-1 and administered CPR , but by the time the paramedics got there, she was gone."

My eyes were dry and my throat burned. I couldn't process the fact that Grace was dead.

"I need to see them."

THE SOUND of toddler chatter woke me. I opened my eyes, and the sight of the two people I loved most in this world together took my breath away. Hailey was sitting on Penny's lap and talking non-stop about something or another. Tears filled my eyes at the thought that I could have lost my baby. I also grieved for the loss of Grace. She'd been my first love. My friend. The mother of my child. And she was gone. Ruthlessly taken from this world by some piece of shit who never deserved her.

I shifted and the noise alerted Penny whose gaze darted up to meet mine. Her smile was sad.

"Hey." That single word was all I could get out.

Hailey's head turned in my direction. "Daddy!"

She slid down and rushed toward me with Penny right behind her calling out a warning. "Gently, sweetie. Remember, your daddy is hurt."

She skidded to a halt and slowed her pace. Carefully, she crawled onto the bed, thankfully on the side without the broken leg, and hugged me. Then she sat up and stared at all the tubes.

"Do you want me to kiss it and make it better?"

Ahh, the innocence of youth. I smiled. "Thank you, baby."

I winced when Hailey's hand pressed on a particularly sore spot as leaned over me and dropped sweet kisses on all my "boo-boos". She sat back with a self-satisfied smile.

"All better now."

I cupped her adorable cheek in my palm. With my free hand, I reached out to grasp Penny's so we were all connected. Her expression made me nervous.

"How are you feeling, really?"

I rubbed my thumb across her knuckles. "Better now that you're here."

She squeezed my hand before pulling away. "Good, I'm glad. I was so worried about you. Do you know I was working in the trauma room when they brought you in?"

I shook my head numbly. "I don't remember much of last night. Or was it the night before? I've been so out of it."

Why didn't you tell me?"

I knew what Penny was asking. I glanced down at the now quiet girl lying on my chest.

"I wasn't sure how. It just never seemed like the right time."

She drew back like I'd punched her. "Never seemed—"

Her voice came out high-pitched and she stopped to clear her throat. When she began again, her tone was measured. "Nevermind. We're not doing this right now. I'm going to let you visit with your daughter. From what I understand you don't see her much. I'll be back in a little bit."

"Pen—"

She cut me off. "Not now, Marcus."

Penny leaned down and smiled at Hailey. "You and your daddy have a nice time together. I'll be back soon and we'll go to the park and play. Okay?"

"Otay, 'enny," she mumbled around the thumb in her mouth.

Without another word, she turned and left me alone with my daughter.

CHAPTER 25

I ALMOST FELT guilty for leaving Marcus. I was pretty sure he was still feeling like shit, but right now, I was in a mood. And I wasn't sure which one exactly.

I was extremely hurt that he hadn't told me he had a daughter. I was also feeling a little insecure, which was dumb. He'd gone to visit Grace last night. I knew he loved me, but did he still have feelings for her? She was the mother of his child, after all. Knowing those thoughts only led down a road I didn't want to take, I pushed them aside. I headed to the waiting room where Bridget sat. She looked up at my entrance.

"Where's the kiddo?"

I sat down next to her. "With her father. I figured Marcus would want to see her. To make sure she's really okay. I'm betting it hasn't really hit him yet what happened. We've had a couple days to process."

She reached out for my hand. "How are you doing? I can't tell you enough how sorry I am that I didn't tell you about Hailey. Honestly, I thought you knew."

I shrugged. "I'll be okay once I get over the hurt. It just stings that he kept such a huge secret from me. I mean, she's his daughter. That's something you really should tell the woman you say you love. I'm probably being unreasonable, but it's so fresh right now."

"Marcus loves you. I don't know his reason for not clueing you in, but I know it wasn't for any malicious reason."

"I know." I glanced at my watch. "I probably better get back in there. I'm sure Marcus needs to get some rest and as chatty as Hailey is, he's most likely fighting to stay awake. I guess I've tortured him long enough. For today, at least."

Bridget chuckled. "Oh, I have no doubt you'll find far more sadistic ways to torture him in the future."

I cocked a half-smile as I rose from the chair. "You're probably right. I'll see you soon?"

She stood as well and hugged me. "Of course. You take care of that man and little girl of yours."

My heart raced at her words. Hailey *was* my little girl now. Her father was mine too. A sliver of happiness overshadowed all the hurt and self-doubt I'd been feeling.

"I will. I'll call you later."

Bridget and I hugged goodbye again, and I made my way back to Marcus' room.

I knocked on the door, let myself in, and stopped in my tracks. The two of them were fast asleep, Hailey on top of her father's chest, her thumb still in her mouth. His arms were wrapped tightly around her like he never wanted to let her go. My heart overflowed with love for the two of them.

The pain also amplified.

I WAS at the hospital after dropping Hailey off at Bridget's.

"Hi. I'd hoped you'd be back tonight."

I closed the door behind me and made my way over to the chair. "I wasn't sure if you'd be sleeping or not."

"Nah, I've been sleeping for two days. I'm too keyed up anyway. I'm ready to get out of this place."

"I think the doctor said you could go home tomorrow or the day after if your tests came back okay. You just have to be patient."

Marcus groaned. "I'm not the most patient person. I'm going stir crazy in here. And my leg aches like a mother fucker."

"You're going to have to clean up your language with a toddler in the house. You know that, right?"

He sighed almost in despair and dropped his head back against the pillow. "I'm going to be terrible at this father thing."

I scoffed. "I doubt that."

He raised his head and stared me right in the eye. "I'm sorry."

I gave a short nod. "I know."

"The truth is, I didn't know how to bring up the topic. I mean, here I was going to great lengths to protect Grace from Evan. I wasn't sure what you'd think if you knew Hailey was part of the package. I didn't want to lose you."

"Why would you lose me? Marcus, I love you."

He sighed. "I didn't want you to think there was something still going on between Grace and me just because we shared a daughter."

"Were you ever going to tell me about her?"

"Of course," he said fiercely. "Once Evan had been dealt with."

"What if that didn't happen? He could have harassed you for months. Maybe years. Would Hailey have been a teenager before I even knew of her existence?"

He slammed his fist down on the mattress. "No. I don't know. Damn it. I don't know what you want me to say."

I sat on the edge of his bed. "I don't want you to say anything. I just want you to understand where I'm coming from. You can't imagine the hurt I felt walking into that house and seeing that little girl, knowing she was a part of you. A part you'd kept hidden from me. It was literally like a punch to the gut. Like you didn't trust me enough to tell me about her. I've opened myself up to you completely, in more ways than one, and all this time you were withholding something, some*one*, that important."

Marcus reached for my hand and clasped it tightly. His voice came out choked. "Jesus, Penny, I'm more sorry than I can say. You're right. I made a mistake. One I wholly regret. Can you please forgive me?"

I leaned down and caressed his cheek. "I love you Marcus. I just need some time."

He turned his head and pressed a kiss to my palm. "I love you too. With everything that I am."

We sat together a little longer, but then I needed to get going.

"I'll bring Hailey back for another visit tomorrow if you aren't released. Then, hopefully you can come home the day after."

"I sure hope so."

I kissed him goodbye and went to pick up my new daughter.

CHAPTER 26

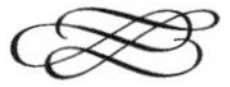

THREE DAYS after Grace had been killed, I'd called her parents. I could still vividly recall the conversation.

"I'm so sorry."

Grace's mother, Martha, broke down at my apology.

Stoic and almost too composed, her father, Thomas, spoke. "What the fuck happened, Marcus? How did Evan find our Grace? I thought she and Hailey were protected. Please explain to me how our daughter can be dead."

I shifted guiltily in my bed. "It's my fault, sir. Evan followed me to the house. He shot her two guards and then, from my understanding, he and Grace fought over the gun, which discharged. I wish I could take everything about that night back."

Neither replied. I filled in the uncomfortable silence. "Her death will be on my conscience for the rest of my life. I can offer nothing but my sincerest apology and deepest sympathy to you and Martha."

"Where's Hailey now?" Thomas asked, ignoring my apology.

"My girlfriend is taking care of her while I'm in the hospital.

She brings her here to visit every day. When I'm well, I want to introduce you to her. It's time she met her grandparents."

"We'd really like that." This came from Martha, who sniffled.

I cleared my throat. "I'd like to take care of the arrangements for Grace, if you'd let me."

Soon after that, with the assurances that all arrangements would be taken care of, I said my goodbyes and promised I'd bring their granddaughter to visit as soon as I could.

That had been almost three weeks ago. Since then, I hadn't slowed down. I dove full force back into work even though it was from home. A home where Hailey now lived. Penny was always on my mind. I knew I'd hurt her and I'd apologized. I'd given her the space and time she requested, but she'd remained closed off. It was time for this stand off to end. We loved each other too much. I made a phone call to the one person I'd wanted to avoid, because I knew I'd get a lecture and I wasn't in the mood.

"Hello?"

"Hey, it's Marcus."

"Yes?" I could literally *hear* the glare in the word.

"I need a favor."

Bridget harrumphed on the other end. "Oh, really? And what sort of favor can I help you with? You need another secret kept?"

I sighed in irritation. "No, I don't need any more secrets kept. I need you to watch Hailey for the night."

"Oh, and why is that?" she asked with a little too much snark.

"Penny and I are going to have a discussion tonight." I might as well explain myself to her, because I knew how Bridget was. Sometimes, it was less painful this way.

"I hope you plan on groveling."

My temper snapped. "I want you to listen and listen well. I've put up with your goddamn attitude and bratty behavior for years now because of what you did for Grace. I understand, and appreciate, your loyalty to Penny, but this bullshit ends now, Bridget. What happens between my submissive and me is off limits and none of your fucking business. If I wanted your commentary, I'd ask for it. Do you understand?"

There was a long pause and then a quiet response. "Yes, Sir."

"Good. Now, are you able to watch Hailey or not?"

"Of course. You can drop her off whenever you need to." Bridget sounded sufficiently chastised.

"Thank you. I'll bring her by around seven. I'll have her fed and in her pajamas and ready for bed."

"Okay, I'll see you then."

I disconnected the call and made plans for tonight.

I RAISED my hand to pound on the door again when it suddenly swung open.

"What do you"—Penny paused mid-sentence—"Marcus, what are you doing here?"

"Do you mind if I come in and sit down? My damn leg is killing me."

Her shocked gaze took me in when I practically pushed my way inside on my crutches.

I made myself comfortable on the couch. She crossed her arms and repeated her question.

"Why are you here?"

I gestured to the space next to me. "Sit, please."

When she tried sitting on the other end, I reached for her hand and pulled her onto my lap.

"Don't move."

Penny froze at the command. I interlaced our fingers, and brushed the hair off her face with my other hand. My eyes zeroed in on her sapphire ones.

"I've given you your space because I know I fucked up and you needed time to process why I didn't tell you about Hailey. Yes, I should have told you, but as I already explained, I didn't really know how. I'd spent so long trying to protect them, that it was just habit for me. I'm sorry for that. But this ends now. I've apologized. It was wrong of me, and it won't happen again. But damn it Penny, you're mine, and I'm not letting you go. I love you. I think I've loved you since the first time I saw you. I want to spend the rest of my life with you. I want Hailey to grow up to be as smart, funny, kind, and beautiful as you are. I want you to wear my ring. I want to spend the rest of my life showing you how much I love you."

With each word I spoke, her eyes widened until finally, they filled with tears. "I know you didn't mean to hurt me. I love you Marcus."

I let go of her hand and with both thumbs brushed the wetness off her cheeks. I cupped her face and leaned ghosted my lips across hers. It had been too long. It felt like coming home.

I feathered kisses across her cheeks, licking away her tears from each eyelid. I moved to her nose before making my way back to her mouth. I deepened the kiss, angling my head so we fit together like two pieces of a puzzle. My tongue swept through her mouth, and her taste was like the finest chocolate.

Penny shifted and I let her. Especially when she moved to straddle my lap, taking care not to jar my injured leg. I gripped her hips and pressed her closer to me. Her chest pressed against mine, and she ran her hands through my hair, tilting my head back to gain more leverage over the kiss. I let her control the tempo.

My hands moved from her hips to her ass, squeezing and kneading her cheeks as we re-learned each other's taste. It had been so long. I drew her pajama top up and over her head before tossing it to the floor. Our mouths met again. We couldn't stop tasting each other. Then kissing was no longer enough.

"I need you inside me now, Sir. Please don't make me wait," she begged.

"Stand up and take your pants off," I ordered.

She practically jumped off me in her haste. While Penny disrobed, I unbuttoned my pants and my cock sprung free. Not wasting another minute, she carefully climbed back in my lap and took my cock in hand, slowly lowering herself down until I was balls-deep inside her. She gasped and threw her head back pushing her breasts forward.

I thrust upward at the same time I leaned forward and took one of her nipples into my mouth and suckled, pulling it taut, applying pressure with my teeth before releasing it with a soft pop. I moved to her other breast, showing it the same attention.

Penny continued moving over me, rubbing her clit across my pelvis. She rocked her body faster and my grip tightened on her ass. Needing her to reach her peak, I slid my finger down her crack, teasing her back hole before wetting the tip of my digit with her juice. Then I moved my finger back up and entered her ass. That was all it took for her orgasm to race through her. She threw her head back and screamed my name as I flooded her pussy with my seed.

Tiny aftershocks continued to pulse around my cock as she fell against my chest, our heartbeats matching rhythms. I pushed her hair off my face and feathered light kisses across her brow.

"I love you, Penny."

"I love you too, Sir," she whispered.

CHAPTER 27

IT HAD BEEN three months since that fateful night. I'd moved in with him and Hailey, and we'd slowly settled into a routine. I'd fully embraced my submissive side, and my Dom and I were exploring more and more of my limits. Tonight, we were at Eden to celebrate my birthday.

Marcus had almost swallowed his tongue when I modeled my outfit for him at the house. I was dressed in a corset of royal blue with black lace accents that accentuated my perfect hourglass figure, according to Bridget, and barely covered my nipples. I completed the outfit with a black leather miniskirt, black fishnet thigh highs with matching garter belt hidden under my skirt, and black peep toe, sling back pumps. Marcus told me he loved the colors since they reminded him of the first time he'd tied me to his bed. I actually felt beautiful in the outfit, and it was a reminder that I was beginning to embrace my body. Before tonight, I never would have worn something like this in public.

Once we reached the public playroom, we headed to

the bar where Marcus helped me up onto the stool. He signaled the bartender.

"I'll have a gin and tonic and whiskey sour, please."

"You got it."

When the waiter left to fill our order, Marcus turned to me.

"I have a surprise for you."

I narrowed my eyes. "Oh?"

His look of innocence didn't fool me one minute. "What, you don't like surprises?"

I crossed my arms on top of the bar and glared suspiciously at him. "Not particularly."

He took one step forward and palmed the back of my head, angling so my neck was exposed. He nuzzled the bare skin with his scruffy jaw and nibbled on my shoulder.

"Oh, I think you'll enjoy this surprise quite a bit."

Just then the waiter returned with our drinks. We sat at the bar drinking and enjoying the public play going on. Quickly, Marcus downed his drink, and before I could finish mine, he took the glass from my hand and set it on the bar top. Then, he wrapped his arm around my waist and pulled me off the stool.

"Hey, I wasn't done with that," I complained, which only earned me a swat on my ass.

"Come with me."

He spoke in my ear, keeping me in close contact at the same time he paraded me through the public play room and toward the back hallway. He walked us down the hall to the second to last room on the right. I stepped inside when he opened the door and took in my surroundings. I heard the snick of the door closing behind me.

Unlike the last room we'd been in, this particular

room was subdued. There was nothing garish or flamboyant about it. It was almost demure, in fact. Candles had been placed randomly around the room, creating a balanced harmony between soft light and deep shadows. A king-size bed with its burgundy plush velveteen coverlet graced the far wall of the room. Two additional pillar candles burned on either side of the wrought iron headboard. A light, aromatic mist scented the room with a hint of lavender and vanilla. It was a room designed for seduction. I stood in the middle of it, taking everything in.

I sighed in pleasure when I felt my hair swept off my back and Marcus placed soft kisses along my ear and neck, nuzzling the sweet spot he knew drove me wild. I tilted my head to give him better access and he deeply inhaled my scent. He continued to rain kisses down my shoulder, unlacing the ribbons of my corset as he went. He plucked at each strand, finally loosening it enough to slide it up and over my head. He dropped it to the floor at almost the same time he turned me toward him and crushed his mouth to mine, biting at my lips.

Without hesitation, I opened to him and our tongues began a familiar dance. Without breaking our kiss, he maneuvered me backwards. When my knees hit the bed, I lost my balance, and we fell backwards onto it, our lips only briefly losing contact before meeting again. I lost track of time.

Marcus pulled back and murmured against my lips. "Scoot up to the top and take off your skirt."

With a sexy smile, I scooted backward with my forearms before lifting my butt and shimmying out of the skirt as he moved to stand next to the bed. I tossed it off to the side and started to unhook my garter belt as well, but his deep voice stopped me.

"I didn't give you permission to remove anything except your skirt. Leave them."

My hands lowered to the bed and I remained still, waiting for the next command while his eyes devoured me.

"Now, touch yourself."

He didn't say anything else as he patiently waited to see if I followed his instruction. Seductively, or at least I hoped that's how I looked, I moved my hands up to cup my breasts. I squeezed them and plucked my nipples, my arousal kicking into higher gear. I moaned at the sensation of my own hands causing me so much pleasure. I watched Marcus through hooded eyes and held back a smile when I noticed the huge tent in his pants.

Wanting to tease him a little, I skimmed one of my hands down the length of my body and slipped it between my legs to rub my clit with my fingertip. My back arched in pleasure when I moved my finger down and barely dipped it into my pussy. I opened my eyes and made eye contact with him. Forest-green had darkened to almost black with passion.

With a cheeky grin, I crooked a finger at him. Not waiting a minute, Marcus quickly undressed and joined me on the bed.

"You're quite the little tease tonight, aren't you?"

He grabbed my hand in his and before I could guess his intent, he pushed my finger deeper, wetness coating our digits. He continued helping me fuck myself before adding his finger alongside mine. My pussy pulsed around the delicious intrusion and I clenched my muscles to try and pull them in further. I was on the precipice of an orgasm when Marcus wrenched our fingers out, stopping it.

I pouted up at him and groaned in frustration. "God, you love to torture me. I was almost there."

He smacked my bared pussy causing me to twitch and moan again in pleasure. "I'm in control here, not you. You should have learned that by now, Sweetness."

With his words, he moved over me, bringing my hands above my head and locking my wrists together as he ground our lips together. I nipped at his bottom lip. In retaliation, he lightly slapped my breast with his free hand, and I writhed beneath him in pleasure. Maintaining hold on my wrists, he opened his mouth and kissed my breast to soothe the sting.

"Grab the headboard,"—Marcus commanded as he released my hands to move further down my body—"and don't let go."

He didn't wait to see if I obeyed as his lips reached my sex. Grabbing my heels, he bent my knees toward my chest and balanced my legs over shoulders. The he dove in to feast, lapping up my cream as he spread me open and plunged his tongue deep inside. I jerked when he withdrew and traced a line down to my anus. He circled the puckered hole before dipping inside as I writhed beneath him. He kept me on edge until I couldn't take it any longer and an orgasm ripped through me. I screamed out Marcus' name and shuddered uncontrollably beneath him, my fingers still gripping the headboard so tightly my knuckles ached.

"I'm proud of you, sub," he praised me as he gently pried my death grip off the iron.

I sighed in satisfaction as my eyes locked on his. "Thank you, Sir. It took everything I had not to let go. I didn't want to disappoint you."

"You did well, Sweetness."

There was a soft knock on the door. When I made to cover myself, Marcus stopped me.

"Enter," he called out, and I tensed slightly.

The door opened and in walked a familiar blond haired man.

"Welcome, Donovan. So glad you were able to join us."

He scanned the scene in front of him, his eyes darkening in arousal as he drank in my nakedness. "Thanks for inviting me. I've been looking forward to this all night. I'm a little disappointed to have missed the appetizer though."

When Donovan stepped into the room, I immediately knew what my "surprise" was. I'd made it clear that a threesome was on my list of soft limits. So, while I was a little shocked, I knew I shouldn't have been. I'd watched him scene many times over the last few months, and any time he saw Marcus and me, he flirted and continually hinted about joining us for an evening of fun. Apparently, tonight was that night. I was certainly attracted to him, and I could admit to being curious about what he looked like naked.

The bed dipped as Marcus lay down next to me, and I arched into the touch as he drew circles around my breast. His voice rasped across my skin enticing me with his words.

"Relax, love. Let us give you pleasure beyond your wildest dreams. Four hands touching you, two pairs of lips kissing you, and most importantly, two cocks filling you. Stop thinking and start feeling. You're a desirable woman, and both of us want to do nothing but pleasure you. Imagine my cock finally inside your ass. Remember, you can always use your safe word. I will never take that away from you."

I pictured the lips and the cocks and all the hands touching me, pleasing me. His reminder of my safe word only made me place my trust more fully in him. I appreciated his reassurance and this was what I wanted.

"Yes, please. I want both of you inside me."

Now that I'd committed to going forward, a boldness I'd never experienced before came over me, and I reached out for Marcus' cock. I needed to taste him, and the longer I waited the harder it was to resist. I leaned up for a kiss at the same time his finger thrust into my sex. Our tongues danced, and I took control. I knew it was only an illusion though. The kiss went on as Marcus continued to pleasure me. When the bed dipped again, I broke our connection in surprise, completely forgetting that Donovan was with us.

While Marcus and I had been occupied, Donovan had taken his clothes off, and my wish was fulfilled. He was pleasantly muscular, with more of a swimmer's build. I also noticed a Marine Corps tattoo with dates and a couple names on the left side of his chest. I only caught a glimpse of his cock before he bent down to touch his lips to mine hesitantly, as though making sure I was okay with it.

I was definitely okay with it. He tasted different than Marcus, of course, but I still enjoyed the flavor. As we learned each other's taste, Marcus shifted his full attention to my pussy. Teeth and tongue played at my clit and I contracted my muscles to try and pull his fingers deeper inside me. The dual sensation of being eaten out while Donovan deepened the kiss, his tongue dancing across the roof of my mouth, was almost overwhelming. When Marcus sucked my entire clit in his mouth I almost exploded off the bed.

Donovan's mouth left mine and trailed downward until he surrounded one breast, pulling the nipple with his teeth. Not wanting to neglect my other breast, he palmed it and tweaked its nipple between his thumb and forefinger. Without thought, I clasped my hands to his head and held him closer, loving the emotions these two men brought out in me. My orgasm simmered right beneath the surface, and any second, it was going to explode across every nerve ending in my body. I chased the feeling, my pussy tightening around Marcus' fingers, ready for the sensation to surround me.

Abruptly, he pulled back, and practically growled.

"Stop."

To my dismay my orgasm receded. My heavy-lidded eyes barely focused on my Dom, and it took all my concentration to see that Donovan had stopped his ministrations and also looked at Marcus. A look passed between the two men, and the air shifted as though something momentous just happened.

Marcus rose to his knees and ordered Donovan to his back. He nodded in assent and positioned himself. I rolled to my side and propped myself up on my elbow to get a closer look at him. His cock was slightly longer than Marcus' but not quite as wide. The veins along the side throbbed, and the purple head was beautifully shaped. I saw something fly past me as he reached up to catch it mid air. He opened his hand to show me the condom. He tore open the wrapper, and I stared as he rolled it on, teasing me with his slow, sensual movements. I squealed in surprise when he grabbed me, pulling me over his body so my legs separated on either side of him, pushing my pussy flush up against his abdomen and reigniting the spark. I undulated against him, rubbing my wetness against him to add friction to my clit that would push me over the edge. I yelped in surprise when Marcus slapped his palm across my ass.

"Not yet, little sub."

I wasn't beyond begging at this point. "I need to come so bad, Sir. Please, let me come again."

Heat spread across my back as Marcus pressed his chest against it. My breasts swelled in his hands as he reached around to cup them. I yelped in surprise when he bit my ear.

"Patience, Sweet. I want you to scream my name when you come."

He released me when Donovan reached up to thread his hands in my hair and pull me down for a kiss. He devoured my mouth and pulled my chest closer, which pushed my ass up in the air. With his hands now free, Marcus moved them to my ass kneading my cheeks and swiping his thumbs up and down my crease, not pressing, but with enough pressure to make me notice. After a few touches, my cheeks were spread open. I felt a brush of air across my asshole, and I jumped in shock when he ran his tongue around my opening before spearing it deep inside.

With one last swipe, he pulled away and rasped in my ear, "I need to be inside your ass right now. Lift up."

I obediently followed his order. Donovan grasped the base of his cock tightly as Marcus slowly lowered me down onto it. I gasped at the sensation of being filled, and my body adjusted to the difference in their size. I writhed and moaned in ecstasy, shifting enough to push him farther up inside me. I rocked against him a few times until Marcus pushed against my back and pressed me downward until my chest was flush with Donovan's again.

With my ass fully up in the air, I waited impatiently for Marcus to finally end my torture. The sound of a drawer opening and closing echoed in the air and a cold wetness touched my back passage. Using two fingers, he coated the outside of my asshole with lube before pressing the same two fingers deep inside, spreading the lube around. He scissored his fingers, opening me wider and wider in preparation for his cock. I needed the distraction, so I leaned against Donovan and thrust my tongue into his mouth, kissing him for all I was worth.

Marcus removed his fingers and my asshole clenched on nothing while my pussy clamped down Donovan's cock. It was greedy to be filled. Luckily, I didn't have to wait long.

"Take a deep breath and when you exhale, push out," Marcus instructed.

Without wasting a second, I inhaled then exhaled and pushed out against his cock. Slowly, the head entered with a pop.

"Oh my God, I'm so full already. I don't think I can take any more," I groaned as the pressure continued to build.

With Donovan inside my cunt and Marcus pushing into my ass, I'd never been so full in my entire life. I was awestruck at the feeling even if I shifted in slight discomfort.

"You can take me, Penny. You can take both of us. Keep

breathing out as I push in," he continued his encouragement as he kept pushing.

Within seconds, I felt his balls brush up against me and I knew he was fully seated. He stopped moving to give me time to get used to the complete and utter fullness.

"Fuck," he exclaimed. "You are amazing. Donovan, you good, man?"

My heart actually ached a little that I had completely forgot about the man beneath me. Even being a part of me as he currently was, it had always been about Marcus.

The vibration of Donovan's chuckle rumbled through me. "Hell yeah, I'm good."

I laughed a little at his response and looked him in the eyes and saw arousal. I also saw that his laughter didn't quite reach them. This wasn't the Donovan I'd come to know over the last few months. I leaned close to whisper in his ear, not wanting Marcus to hear, "Are you okay?"

Surprise flickered in his eyes. He smiled, but it seemed forced. "I'm fine. How could I not be with a beautiful woman fucking my brains out?"

I knew he deflected my question, but decided to let it go. Now wasn't the time.

"If you two are done up there, can we keep moving this along? I have my dick up my gorgeous sub's ass, and I'm ready to fuck."

I choked out a laugh. "Yes, Sir. I'm ready."

"Thank God."

He started moving and I forgot about my previous conversation. Marcus pulled out so only the tip was in and pushed forward again. After a few thrusts, Donovan caught the rhythm and they began a coordinated dance where Donovan thrust in, Marcus pulled back, and as

Marcus pushed in, Donovan pulled back. Back and forth, they pushed my pleasure higher than it had ever been until, as Marcus predicted, I screamed his name as my orgasm exploded through me, followed closely by Donovan. Marcus continued thrusting until he threw his head back with his orgasm and his seed filled me up.

Complete exhaustion overcame me, and I collapsed against Donovan's chest, unable to move an inch. Marcus pulled out and the bed shifted as he rose from it. His feet tapped on the floor, and soon I heard running water. He returned with a warm cloth and cleaned me while I continued to lie there. The bed dipped and he pulled me against him with my back to his front. I snuggled into his warmth and my eyes grew heavy. When the bed listed again, it was from Donovan leaving it.

He leaned down and brushed a kiss over my forehead. "Thank you for letting me help you celebrate your birthday."

I murmured sleepily. "Thank you for making this one of my best birthdays ever."

I barely heard the snick of the door closing before I was fast asleep.

CHAPTER 28

AFTER BRIEFLY DOZING LAST NIGHT, I'd woken Penny up and taken her home. Today though, I had one final birthday present for her. I was in the kitchen finishing making breakfast when she dropped onto her chair with a yawn.

"Good morning, love. Did you sleep all right?"

She took a sip from her glass of orange juice. "Most definitely."

"I'm glad." I plated our omelets and brought them to the table.

We both started eating, and she moaned her approval. "This tastes so good. Thank you for making breakfast."

"You're welcome."

We continued our meal before I broke the silence. "Do you have any plans for the day?"

Penny shook her head. "Just a quick errand, but other than that, no. Why?"

"I want to take you and Hailey on a picnic this afternoon."

She smiled. "I'd love that."

After finishing our meal, she helped me clean the kitchen before heading upstairs to shower. I let her know I was going to go pick up Hailey.

I parked in front of the condo and trekked up the walk before knocking on the door. Moments later, it was opened by a gentleman in his early 60s. "Is Bridget here?"

The man stepped back and gestured for me to enter. "Come on in. You must be Hailey's dad."

Who the hell was this guy?

"Brian Carter, Bridget's father."

I took his offered hand. "Oh, it's a pleasure to meet you sir."

"You as well. My daughter has told me a lot about you. I'm sorry for Hailey's, and your, loss."

"Thank you."

Just then Bridget entered the living room with Hailey in tow. Her eyes lit up when she saw me standing there.

"Daddy!"

She rushed forward, her short little legs quickly eating up the space between us, and dove into my arms. She peppered my face with kisses and I hugged her tight. I glanced up to see both Bridget and her father looking at me with matching sorrowful expressions, holding each other's hand. When they caught my glance, they both smiled like nothing was going on.

"Thanks for watching Hailey again for us."

She released her father's hand and wrapped her arms around her. "Anytime. She's a lot of fun. Let me grab her stuff and I'll be right back."

Turning quickly, she headed down the hall. I glanced at her dad whose eyes followed her retreat. His face was downcast, and he suddenly looked so sad standing there. He turned and cleared his throat.

"Your daughter is adorable. She certainly doesn't know a stranger," he chuckled.

"Thank you," I said with pride.

Bridget returned with Hailey's overnight bag and handed it to me. We said our goodbyes and we headed out to the car. From there, we ran our own errand. When we got home, Penny was still out, so I spent daddy/daughter time having an extremely important conversation.

I DROVE through the city park, the sunlight creating dappled designs on the road as it peeked through the trees running parallel on each side of the road. Hailey was chattering in her carseat in the back while Penny looked around. When I finally parked, and exited the car, she followed suit, while I lifted my daughter out. I grabbed the picnic basket as well when she tried to reach for it.

"I got it. You just follow us."

We walked together until we reached the familiar shelter house. I placed the basket on the table and set Hailey down. She immediately took off toward the small playground a few yards from where we stood. I pulled Penny into my arms, her back to my front, continuing to keep a watchful eye on our daughter.

"Do you recognize this place?" I nuzzled her neck.

She laid her arms over mine on her waist and angled her head. "Of course I do. This is where we met."

I dropped a kiss on her shoulder before turning her to face me.

"That was the best day of my life."

She raised up on tippy toes and pressed her lips against me. "Mine too. I love you."

"Come on, let's eat."

I called Hailey over and she crawled into Penny's lap. I handed Hailey a sandwich bag filled with cheese puffs. While I kept digging for the rest of our lunch, she suddenly stopped eating.

"Penny?"

"Yes, baby?" she replied, looking down at the little girl in her arms.

Hailey reached into the bag and pulled something out. "Daddy told me to give this to you."

She turned her hand over and in her palm lay a small piece of tissue paper. Penny looked up at me as she gingerly took the offering. She looked back down and slowly unwrapped the folded material. Gasping, her hand covered her mouth. Her eyes met mine again, this time, hers filled with tears.

"I love you, Penny Stephens. Will you marry me?"

She nodded frantically as the tears fell.

Hailey shifted in her lap and patted her cheek. "Why you crying?"

"Because I'm so happy."

I leaned over and took the ring from her hand, placing it on her shaking finger. I pressed my lips to hers and the sound of my giggling daughter had us breaking apart.

Later that night, after Hailey had been put to bed, I made my way down the stairs and into the living room to find Penny sitting on the couch admiring her ring. I sat next to her and pulled her against me.

"I'm so happy," she said as she glanced up at me. "I've

suddenly gotten everything I ever wanted in life. I only hope I don't wake in the morning to find this all a dream."

I kissed her forehead. "Sorry, you're not going to get rid of me so easily. You're stuck with me for life now."

"I think I can handle that."

She rose from the couch and held out her hand. I clasped it in mine and we headed to our room, where I proceeded to show her how much I loved her.

EPILOGUE

I'd been waiting for this day for six months. Six months in which my life had changed in ways I'd only ever dreamed. I never thought I would be a wife and a mother, and now I was both. I'd never considered myself particularly religious, but I thanked God every day for Marcus and Hailey, who had become the family I'd always wanted, but never thought I'd have.

She still asked for Grace, but was too young to understand that her mom wasn't coming back. We tried explaining that she was in heaven, but Hailey didn't fully grasp the concept. In the meantime, we were going to make sure she knew how much her mom loved her. When she was old enough we'd tell her the entire truth. Until then, I planned on being the best mom ever.

Immediately after Marcus asked me to marry him, we flew to meet Hailey's grandparents. Initially, it was an awkward meeting between the adults, but before the week was over, the four of us had relaxed. I liked Grace's parents very much, and Marcus and I promised we'd make sure they got frequent visits from their granddaughter.

Today, though, my whole focus was on the man waiting for me just down the hall.

As soon as I was alone, I walked over to the full-length mirror. I stared in awe at the beautiful stranger in front of me. Blinking rapidly to clear my vision, I gave a little twirl and watched my train swirl around and settle like the gossamer wings of a butterfly around my legs, making me feel like a fairy princess. I had never truly felt more beautiful than I did today. I wanted to capture this feeling and hold it inside me forever. I heard the music queue up when there was a light knock on the door.

"Are you sure you don't want to run away with me instead?" Donovan joked as he wrapped me in his arms for a giant bear hug. He pulled his head back slightly to smack a wet kiss on my cheek.

I playfully pushed him away and swatted his chest.

"Get real, Casanova." I gestured to my body. "You couldn't handle all of this by yourself. Besides, I'd harsh the hot bachelor vibe you have going on. All the ladies out there are going to swoon after you. They all want to be the one to finally bring you to heel. Besides, Marcus would kick your ass."

Donovan straightened his tie as he inspected me from head to toe. "You're a beautiful bride, Penny. Marcus is lucky to have you. I'm honored you chose me to walk you down the aisle."

"Damn it, Donovan, you're going to make me cry." I groaned.

"C'mon beautiful, let's go get you married."

He lead me out of the room, my train billowing behind

us. As we made our way to the double doors separating me from the love of my life, I recalled my first meeting with Marcus. The butterflies. The sweaty palms. The racing heart. The urge to run. I realized how much I'd changed. I wasn't nervous about the wedding, because the only place I wanted to run was into his arms. I was strong, confident, and as the doors opened to my future, I held my head up high.

The only thing that was the same was how the minute my eyes connected with Marcus' where he stood at the end of the aisle, amazingly sexy in his tuxedo, everyone disappeared except him. There were only the two of us. Like that first day, his eyes devoured me. I put one foot in front of the other and proudly marched toward my man, my Dominant, my Sir. Not once since I entered the sanctuary had his eyes left mine. Our connection was palpable.

When I reached the dais, Marcus took my hand from Donovan's, and as he grasped both of my hands in his, I stared in awe at this man in front of me. Not one for protocol, he pulled me close and brushed a soft kiss across my lips. It was a sweet, lingering kiss that quickly deepened with passion and was filled with love. The delicious and familiar taste of him burst on my tongue. He pulled away, took my hands in his again, and smiled down at me.

"Thank you for not giving up on us. I can't wait to grow old with you, have babies with you, and I'm the luckiest son of a bitch to be able to call you mine. I love you with all my heart."

With a discreet cough, the minister gathered our attention, and without any further interruptions, proceeded with the words that would bind us together.

Forever.

THANK you so much for reading **SUBMISSION**. Whether you loved it or hated it, it would be amazing if you would please leave a review on BookBub or your favorite retailer. Reviews are the lifeblood of an author. They help by spreading word about the book and improving visibility so others have the opportunity to read it. In this world of ever increasing self-published authors, visibility is paramount.

WANT A FREE SHORT STORY? Be sure to sign up for her newsletter and download your copy of A Birthday Spanking, a Doms of Club Eden prequel! http://eepurl.com/ds5MOb

Turn the page for a sneak peek at Desire, book 2 in the Doms of Club Eden series.
Buy it today or read it for FREE in Kindle Unlimited.
Click here: http://amzn.to/2klCPBp

DESIRE

"I NEED YOUR HELP."

My whole body froze at the sound of the voice that haunted my dreams. Slowly, I raised my eyes from the papers scattered across my desk, schooling my features when I saw the stunning redhead standing at my office door. She fidgeted nervously in the doorway looking more beautiful than any woman had a right to. She was tall and all legs with enough curves to draw a man's attention. Long red locks cascaded down her back to dust the top of her ass. Blunt bangs framed her heart-shaped face, and her long lashes made her chocolate brown eyes appear large in her face, but not big enough to disguise the dark circles under them.

She also possessed an energy about her that instantly put me on high alert. I never expected to see Bridget Carter fidget. She always exhibited a self-assuredness that made me envious. I'd never seen her less than confident and bold as brass. Until today. Today, the boldness she typically displayed was missing. Nervousness, and perhaps even a little fear, had taken its place. As the owner of one of the top security and protection firms in the city, this was an expression I saw far too often.

"Bridget, please, come in and have a seat," I directed her as I rose from my chair. She closed the door behind her and made her way to the chair in front of my desk. I walked around the opposite side of my desk and propped my butt on it. She sat on the edge of her chair as if poised to flee quickly. It made me want to slay whatever demons were haunting her. And she definitely appeared haunted. "Now, tell me what you need my help with."

Her breasts distracted me briefly when she inhaled deeply, causing them to rise toward me. I shook myself mentally and brought my focus back to where it needed to be. After a minute, she continued to remain silent. I resisted the urge to reach out to comfort her. Being able to touch her was not something I was ready for, because I knew one touch wouldn't be enough. I typically used a soft, gentle voice when my cases brought me in contact with scared women and kids, but somehow, I knew I needed a different approach. I had observed Bridget often, and closely enough, at the BDSM club we both frequented, I knew how best to get her to respond. In my most firm Dom voice, I tried again. "Tell me what you need, Bridget. Now."

She startled, seeming to forget I stood less than three feet from her. However, my command broke through her thoughts, because she began to speak although still not making eye contact.

"I have a son," she said in a hushed voice, causing my mouth to fall open. Nothing Bridget said could have shocked me more. "Well, biologically, he's my son," she continued. "I gave him up for adoption years ago. I was only a kid myself, and I wanted him to have a better life than I would have been able to give him. I asked for an open adoption because, even though I couldn't take care of him, I still wanted to know he was okay. They sent me regular letters and pictures, but I never initiated contact, and I rebuffed every attempt his adoptive parents made for any type of visitation."

She fidgeted again, shifting slightly in the chair. Her voice quavered as she spoke. "Please don't judge me. Seeing him in person and hearing him call another woman 'mom' would have pushed me over the edge. The decision to give him up almost killed me. But it was a decision I had to make, even knowing I'd only be a part of his life peripherally."

She paused, as if gathering her thoughts, before she continued. "I left the option open that he be allowed access to my information when he turned eighteen. He's only thirteen, so I assumed if he had any interest in contacting me, it wouldn't be for another five years. Except two days ago, I received a phone call. It only lasted a few seconds, and I don't even know if it was really him. I only heard, 'I think you're my mother. Please, help me,' and then a scuffle in the background before the line went dead."

Bridget stopped speaking and finally raised her eyes to meet mine. What I saw in them gutted me. Unable to resist touching her any longer, I moved from my perch and knelt at her feet. I laid one hand on top of hers, which she had been wringing in her lap. Then, I reached up with my other hand to wipe away the lone tear that traced a path down her cheek. "I need you to tell me everything."

I told my assistant to hold all my calls, and for the next

hour, Bridget explained to me that, right before she'd turned sixteen she discovered she was pregnant. Her mom died when Bridget was young, so her father raised her. He worked two jobs to support them, and when she became pregnant she knew there was only one option. She located an adoption agency and found the perfect adoptive family. Immediately after the birth of the baby, Bridget turned him over to them without even seeing him, because she thought it would be easier not to become attached. The adoptive parents made multiple attempts throughout the years to initiate contact, but Bridget never felt ready. The only information she was able to provide were their names and the return address used on the mail she'd received from them. "Connor, what if it was Alex? Why would he be calling me and not his parents? Especially asking for help. He sounded scared. Please, can you help me? I don't know where else to turn."

I instinctively knew helping Bridget would test me like nothing before. Not only because I might be a little in love with her, but because something deep inside told me this case would bring forth demons I'd fought hard to bury. But this wasn't about me. It was about Bridget, and God knew I would move heaven and Earth to find and destroy anything that threatened her or anyone she cared about.

ONCE BRIDGET LEFT, I sat in my office contemplating everything she'd told me. I started my own security and protection firm, Blacklight Securities, eight years ago after busting my ass to rise above all the bad shit in my past. I wanted to be in a position where I could help people who didn't know where to turn. People like my mother. When I opened my doors for business, there were no employees beyond me. After the first year, the company had grown enough for me to hire a couple of associates. By the third year, over twenty men and women were in my employ. I continued to keep my employee list small, but on occasion, I hired an independent contractor for special cases.

I'm a member of an exclusive BDSM club called Club Eden where I met fellow Dominant, Donovan Jeffries. Donovan is a lawyer, and former military. He put me in contact with some of his sources in the government, and I lucked out in getting several high paying government contracts. Most of our cases involve protecting a visiting dignitary or his family, but on occasion, we're hired for personal protection by wealthy businessmen.

My company is also known for taking on cases most other security companies have passed on. Mostly because they thought they were too dignified to be hired for what essentially amounted to high paying babysitting gigs. These jobs certainly weren't ideal, but beggars couldn't be choosers. Now though, we are able to pick and choose our own cases. I also do occasional pro bono work for one of the local battered women's shelters. If only my mother could see me now.

Luckily, I'm currently in between cases. Not that it would have mattered. I would have dropped everything the second the words asking for help crossed Bridget's lips. From here on out my main focus would be on Bridget and her son. *Her son!* I was still in shock by this bombshell she'd dropped. That she had a child was the last thing I would have thought she would tell me. I wasn't sure how I felt about it yet, but it didn't matter. I would have dropped everything the second the words asking for help crossed Bridget's lips. The first thing I needed to find out was who'd made that phone call. And if it was Alex, where were his parents? And why did he sound desperate for help?

Want a FREE short story? Be sure to sign up for my newsletter and download your copy of A Birthday Spanking, a Doms of Club Eden prequel! http://eepurl.com/ds5MOb

AVAILABLE IN KINDLE UNLIMITED

Doms of Club Eden

Submission

Desire

Redemption

Protect

Betrayal

My Christmas Dom

Covert Liaisons Series

Love Undercover

Striking Distance (Coming 2019)

Atonement (Coming 2020)

Other Books

SEALs in Love

Say Yes

ABOUT THE AUTHOR

LK Shaw is a traveling physical therapist assistant by day and author by night. When she isn't traveling for work, she resides in South Carolina with her high maintenance beagle mix dog, Miss P. An avid reader since childhood, she became hooked on historical romance novels in high school. She now reads, and loves, all romance sub-genres, with dark romance and romantic suspense being her favorite. LK enjoys traveling and chocolate. Her books feature hot alpha heroes and the strong women they love.

Want a FREE short story? Be sure to sign up for her newsletter and download your copy of A Birthday Spanking, a Doms of Club Eden prequel! http://eepurl.com/ds5MOb

LK loves to interact with readers. You can follow her on any of her social media:

LK Shaw's Club Eden: https://www.facebook.com/groups/LKShawsClubEden

Author Page: www.facebook.com/LKShawAuthor
Author Profile: www.facebook.com/AuthorLKShaw
IG: @LKShaw_Author
Amazon: amazon.com/author/lkshaw
Bookbub: https://www.bookbub.com/authors/lk-shaw
Website: www.lkshawauthor.com

Made in the USA
Columbia, SC
30 September 2019